ABOVE INSTINCT

ABOVE INSTINCT

James Walker

ARCHWAY
PUBLISHING

Copyright © 2022 James Walker.

All rights reserved. No part of this book may be used or reproduced by any means, graphic, electronic, or mechanical, including photocopying, recording, taping or by any information storage retrieval system without the written permission of the author except in the case of brief quotations embodied in critical articles and reviews.

This is a work of fiction. All of the characters, names, incidents, organizations, and dialogue in this novel are either the products of the author's imagination or are used fictitiously.

Archway Publishing books may be ordered through booksellers or by contacting:

Archway Publishing
1663 Liberty Drive
Bloomington, IN 47403
www.archwaypublishing.com
844-669-3957

Because of the dynamic nature of the Internet, any web addresses or links contained in this book may have changed since publication and may no longer be valid. The views expressed in this work are solely those of the author and do not necessarily reflect the views of the publisher, and the publisher hereby disclaims any responsibility for them.

Any people depicted in stock imagery provided by Getty Images are models, and such images are being used for illustrative purposes only. Certain stock imagery © Getty Images.

ISBN: 978-1-6657-1654-3 (sc)
ISBN: 978-1-6657-1653-6 (hc)
ISBN: 978-1-6657-1655-0 (e)

Library of Congress Control Number: 2022901126

Print information available on the last page.

Archway Publishing rev. date: 01/21/2022

'The First God stepped forward, and in his footprint, our universe began. As the print reflects its maker, in time, his impression filled our universe with new gods, and turned the inanimate into life, and brought man and animal up from the soil.

'Into this divine world we came, too fragile to master it, too simple to understand it. We feel divinity in our minds and see it in nature, but we can never understand the gods nor see our world truly. We feel something greater in our existence, despite how easily living breaks and kills us.

'In this world there is death and suffering, for we are mortals in a divine world. But by surviving, we become stronger, more godlike, and beget stronger generations. You must survive and grow and father, and one day, our descendants will greet the gods as equals.'

—**A father to his two sons.**

ONE

THE WINTER GOD WAS weakening; his bitterness gradually retreating under brightening and clearing skies. Occasional snowfall glided overhead, but the blizzards and snowstorms slept, persuading Follows that travel was safe.

Winter's imprisonment had made him restless. Without conversation or much activity, his own company had grown increasingly difficult. Finally, desperate to escape the overfamiliar surroundings and encouraged by the warming winds, he left his winter caves.

Under weak sunlight he sprang across thinning snows, discarding the stresses of confinement, optimistic and thoughtful. He walked under evergreens heavy with snowfall, watching the waking world. He saw herds of deer traverse the horizon, warm silhouettes against the sky, dawdling and lazy. He watched great snowy plains churned by countless bison, and a lone bear wander searchingly across empty white land. Deprived of much stimulation for a season, each sight was captivating.

The sun arced across the sky as he crossed mountain and valley, each covered horizon further reviving his spirit. When the Sun God retired to rest and the Night God swept clear the heavens, he settled amongst his furs, his mood lifted, tired eyes watching the stars until dreams replaced thoughts. When he woke, he beat on: navigating, hunting, and sheltering. Days and nights passed gently overhead, the weather kind, his wandering and hunting relaxed and easy.

One morning, Follows strode onto a ridge, enjoying the strengthening sun, calm and reflective. But alarm stopped him, silhouetting him against the winter sky overlooking a snowy plain below. He stared across the silent, snow-laden lowland at the two men watching him. Follows remained still, encountering other humans a sobering rarity. Stiffened by his intrusion into their territory, the men inspected him indecisively, burdened with the responsibility of challenging him, but hesitant to risk the confrontation.

Three hundred paces separated the men, all attempting to interpret each other's intentions. Snowflakes whisked on gentle winds between the men, their flight unnoticed and their surroundings severe. No birdsong or movement disturbed the tension; the uncomfortable quiet reigned unchallenged, infecting Follows with nervousness.

Burying his unease, Follows studied the men. One had seen about sixteen winters, his beard thin and broadness youthful. The other man was older, his beard thick, his body strong and dangerous.

He knew the two men were in a difficult situation: they could not allow him to leave without risking their safety. His presence left them susceptible to his ambushes and raids, and their tracks informed Follows of their movements, which could lead him to their camp. Yet a direct assault, despite their outnumbering him, was a dangerous commitment—he was a fully grown male and potentially lethal.

Follows' fear was diluted by two summers and two winters without human contact. Where there were men, there were usually women, and that mere thought was weakening. His desire twisted his stomach and clouded his mind, deterring him from fleeing the area. These men stood between him and a partner; if he could kill them and locate their women, he could end his loneliness.

He tried to ignore the longing threatening his judgement so he could concentrate on forming a plan. He could not directly attack the men: outnumbered, his survival was unlikely; in open ground, he was too vulnerable. Attempting to befriend the men risked their temperament, and their reaction was too unpredictable to chance. They would not speak his language, and they would not risk their lives attempting communication when killing him would ensure their survival. Only his death guaranteed them safety; in their situation, he would attack.

He had no choice but to withdraw and let them hunt him, and then hopefully he could gain an advantage in the woodland behind him. If he could ambush them, he would kill the older man first. He stepped backwards, watching the men. The older man disclosed nothing, but the younger man stepped slowly towards him. The laboured steps betrayed suppressed aggression—the men would pursue.

Follows backed out of sight behind the hill, then ran for the woodland. He sprinted into the wood, tearing amongst the trees looking for places that could lend him an advantage. He judged the men would now be in pursuit, committed to his killing.

He searched wildly for any opportunity to confuse them, frantically inspecting undergrowth, rocks, and hills, until finally an opportunity arose: a downed evergreen collapsed behind a series of closely knit trees. He sprinted a hundred paces past it, then half-circled, now running parallel with his original route towards the fallen fir. He threw himself behind the tree and dug himself into the snow. He focused, his senses tuned to the woodland, listening for his hunters.

He calmed his heavy breathing, buried his winter breaths in his furs, and tightly gripped his spear. He forced himself patient, fighting his shaking. He peered underneath the raised trunk, through its pine needles, at the path he had entered upon. His teeth clenched, the wait frustrated; his mind paced.

He suppressed his fear that he had been outmanoeuvred. The men would not try to flank him: they could too easily lose him and his trail, or unexpectedly emerge into direct contact and lose a chase's forewarning. They would not try to hunt him later, as darkness would hide his tracks and increase their own vulnerability. They would not return to camp for reinforcements, as this allowed him to escape, hide, and stalk them. He steadied his impatience, knowing the men would follow, and if they decided against chasing him, he would track and investigate their group for women later.

Finally, the men came fast across the snow, trailing his footprints, examining their surroundings for any signs. The younger man led; the older man followed. Their breath streamed into the air as they descended upon his footprints, both wearing violence. Despite their caution, they passed him, committing their gravest mistake.

Follows waited two breaths, then stood, stepped soundlessly around the fallen tree, and hurled his spear at the older man. The spear collided into the older man's back, crashing him into the ground, spasms rippling through his failing body. The older man's scream echoed through the trees as Follows sprinted towards the men.

The younger man turned towards the cries and saw his companion impaled and crippled in the snow. Beyond him charged the man responsible. The younger man roared with mixed hate and fear and launched his spear at Follows.

Follows had anticipated the attack and dived into the ground, avoiding the spear. Undeterred, the younger man tore towards Follows, past his struggling and dying companion, his wild eyes promising a brutal confrontation. The two men hurtled into each other and hatefully ripped each other from their feet. They smashed into the ground, punching, clawing, and strangling. The young man tore at Follows' eyes, but he deflected the attack and clasped the young man to his chest. Locked in embrace, the men ruthlessly attacked and brutalised each other, but their closeness disallowed either man space for decisive strikes. The young man grabbed Follows' hair and wrenched his head onto the ground. Follows gripped the young man's throat and strangled him, but the young man pulled himself closer and bit Follows' neck. The pain was immediate but Follows supressed panic, knowing that relinquishing control would advantage the young man. Realising he was losing and that he might die, terror consumed Follows, summoning wild cruelty.

Follows sought the young man's face and pushed his fingers into his eyes. The young man pulled away to knock aside Follows' arm, giving Follows the opportunity he needed. He smashed his fist into the young man's jaw, knocking him backwards, then he leapt upon him, punching and tearing.

The young man tried thrashing free, but his senses were dissolving; he was beaten, his consciousness darkening and deserting him. Follows continued beating the young man—his coherence lost amidst fear and anger—but when he finally realised the boy was dead, his violence faded. As sense returned, he dropped the mauled boy and walked towards the older man.

The older man was alive but motionless, coldly watching him approach. Follows did not hate these men, their circumstances and conflicting interests had demanded the confrontation, not their feelings. But now he needed to ensure they could not call for help. Follows picked up the old man's spear and drove it through his neck, prying him from the world.

Follows collapsed into the snow, distraught, but relieved to have survived. He lay trembling, overwhelmed by fervour, inhaling cold air deep into his starved chest, watching his exhalations flood heavenwards and disappear into the aether. He felt blood seeping beneath his furs and washing over his damp skin. He touched his neck and felt the blood. He fought away his exhaustion and rose; he needed to distance and mend himself. The men's absence would eventually cause concern amongst their family and provoke a search—he could not chance another fight.

Before he fled, he discarded his damaged furs, then retrieved the men's spears and the younger man's clothes. While dressing, he noticed the men's similarities, evidently father and son, suggesting they were from a small family group and that little protection remained for their women.

When ready, he strode into the woods, deepening until a fire's smoke could rise beyond the notice of anyone outside the trees. He disorderly littered his tracks, leaving broken trails to confuse any possible pursuers. Finally, he stopped, judging his surroundings sufficient to hide a fire.

Overhead, winter's early dusk slowly intruded, spilling darkness onto the blue skies and stealing the light beneath the woodland canopy. He moved swiftly inside the shadowing underwood, retrieving tinder and kindling from his pack, and breaking dry branches to fit his hearth. He ground wood together until it smouldered and ignited the tinder, trickling flame onto the kindling, bark, and wood. He warmed a spearhead beside the fireplace to ready its edge to burn his neck. He pressed snow into the cut, cleaning it and slowing the bleeding, numbing it for the searing. He retrieved the spearhead and plunged its edge into his ripped skin.

Experience had familiarised—but never accustomed him—to the agony. His body was littered with scars, disclosing his history of conflict, accidents, and injuries. He sang his cries into his furs, gagging his pain, tears brimming his eyes. He singed himself two further times, ensuring the wound was burnt closed and that he would not bleed into unconsciousness. Dazed by pain, he feebly cleaned his neck with snow, soothing the pain that would linger for days. Cleaning the wound stopped poisonous spirits entering him, avoiding the fatal sickness which can follow injury. He had seen men succumb to this infection, delirious and robbed of lucidity before feverishly dying, like his brother.

He sat panting as he reclaimed composure. His gaze fell into the fire, its swaying entrancing and soothing. His breathing gradually slowed, and equanimity returned, restoring his focus. He returned to his situation. There were probably more men out there, and soon the absent father and son would provoke their search. The invading night might delay them until morning, but nothing was certain. Still, his longing for female company conquered his caution and dissuaded him from fleeing; his loneliness had been growing increasingly difficult over the past seasons.

He extinguished the flames and scattered the fireplace to hide his visit. He retraced his route, keeping away from his already trodden paths, until he returned to the dead father and son. Under fading light, he trailed their footprints past the clearing where he had first encountered the men. Overhead, the Moon emerged through the thinning sky to watch over the frozen world. She invited stars to grace the thickening night and accompany her across the darkening firmament. The tired Sun God fell behind the horizon and left the heavens for the Night God.

The men's trail led Follows into woodland, and he advanced quietly, eyes vigilant and ears attentive. The trees swallowed him under their dusky awnings, their corridors breached by shards of fading crimson light. Then alarm stopped him. The men's tracks diverged from seven sets of footprints, all adult men, ending his hopes for women. Despite his desire and desperation, he knew only swift escape could save him now; his choice was death or flight.

He began withdrawing, his ruined hopes—and his return to isolation—were bitter thoughts. He traipsed morosely outside the trees, the sun now gone and the world moonlit and still. He gathered his bearings from the emerging stars and resumed his route, fortunately away from the men's footprints. Under starry guidance he paced, expeditiously extricating himself from threat.

Soon the group would investigate the absent father and son, but the night would hide his tracks and stall the chase until the Sun

God woke. He would flee through the winter night and distance himself inside its darkness. When first light appeared and the manhunt began, he would be beyond apprehension.

In a few days he could temper his escape, knowing that even the enraged and vengeful would eventually accept their chase's futility and abandon pursuit. He strode through the night, bracing against the cold, stiff against the wind. The starlight coloured the dark lands in grey hues, lighting him a path into the shadows.

TWO

EIGHT UNEVENTFUL DAYS OF flight passed until finally Follows was confident of his safety, allowing him to relax his pace. The father and son faded into the past, and the present reoccupied him, refocusing him on his journey.

The recent days had been kind and temperate, which was summer's gift. Birdsong celebrating the disappearing cold crept into his days, inspiriting his travel and creating a camaraderie with the birds. He whistled to thank them for their music and conversation, hoping to encourage their continued company. Unlike other animals, birds were never wary of him, probably because his kind presented them little danger.

His affinity with animals never diminished, and the privilege of their company never faded. He hunted them through necessity but respected them. Sometimes watching animals relaxed him and postponed his loneliness. Often, he could discern their social dynamics and thoughts, making him feel inexplicably closer to them.

He exhaled contentedly as he watched the birds drift overhead, envying their flight and wishing to similarly soar above the lands that bound him. Each animal usually reminded him of his limitations, making him covet their speed, strength, and imperviousness to cold. He had travelled enormous distances during his lifetime but observed only one creature of similar limitation, the Neanderthal. No other beast wore the hides of another, used weapons, traps, tools, and fires, or was so vulnerable without these protections. But although man had many inadequacies, his endurance was unrivalled, and this won him his contests and sustenance.

He imagined human strangeness attracted other animals' curiosity, but when the birds sang, he felt accepted and invited to enjoy their music despite his oddity. He worried that not understanding their language made him appear unfriendly, but he hoped they recognised his ignorance instead of concluding him insolent.

Despite comparing poorly with other animals, he had seen man beat their strongest and largest. The conquests filled him with pride, for they evidenced man's strength. He had watched the world's confident giants, such as the mammoth and rhino, tricked and felled by his kinsmen. He had seen the great predators, such as the lion and tiger, succumb to man's traps. He knew his kind were not defenceless, and he wanted to claim equality with the gods' strongest creations, but he knew this was untrue.

Many united men were a formidable force, but singularly they were vulnerable. Alone, he was at the world's mercy and fragile against the weather and predators. He remembered his father's words: 'thank the animals that eat from the earth, for if they hunted man, there would be no man.'

Man was a pack animal, driven together to survive, unlike the great predators that roamed alone, needing no communal support to thrive. He knew these creatures lived more freely and less fearfully than humans, for even man's weapons, traps, and cunning were often ineffectual against his larger neighbours. He admired and understood the great predators and knew how to avoid and survive their company; only humans and their unpredictability frightened him.

He thought humans were like wolves, ill-equipped to survive

without a group. They hunted in numbers, combining their efforts and sharing their kills. Together they were fearsome; individually they were weak—even he had triumphed over lone wolves. He judged their kinds equally matched, earning wolves his sympathy.

While Follows walked, he ate dried meats from his pack without pause, ambitious to cover distance. The world insisted anything edible was a staple whether grubs, plants, eggs, insects, animals, birds, or fish; and through lesson, experience and practise he had become an adept procurer of each.

He had killed many animals for their meat and hides, but never maliciously. Often, protracted hunts intimately familiarised him with his prey, teaching him their character and habits. He came to respect his prey, and regretted his survival required their death. Sometimes when a hunt neared its conclusion, the exhausted animal stopped retreating and accepted defeat, hauntingly still and waiting for its end. Its acceptance of death saddened him most; his energies drained witnessing the broken spirit of an animal he admired. But survival always justified the kill.

He had discerned a delicate balance between the species which restrained a champion creature from emerging. Each animal's strength was accompanied by limitation: wolves did not use weapons, tigers hunted alone, man was slow and delicate against the weather. His profound realisation let him glimpse the gods' design which protected each species. Logic defended his conclusion, as the world had existed since the first stars, yet no single animal dominated everywhere.

When he discovered these truths, he felt endowed with divine knowledge and empowered to better tackle life. His insights made him feel closer to the gods and their plans, and perhaps made them notice his growing understanding and astuteness with respect and approval.

Light winds carried through his long hair, coolly stroking his bearded face and skin and inviting his smile. He greeted his closest companion, the Wind God, the most powerful god and his greatest ally. He imagined the birds also sang praise to the Wind God for the winds that raised them above the earth.

Relaxed by the sympathetic weather, he sang to himself and the birds, his songs cheerful company across the snowy flats and hills. The Sun God rolled across the skies scattering faint heat, his strength improving, but presently still delicate. The Winter God's influence was visibly receding, promising to allow summer, its remembered warmth and abundance uplifting.

He understood why the world was torn between the two seasons—his mother had told him the story when he was half his height. The Winter God and Sun God were enemies locked into an eternal conflict that allowed no victor. Their continuous battle had raged throughout time as each god strived to paint the world to their aesthetic. The gods would defeat each other and sculpt the land and skies, only to fatigue and fall to their rested and rejuvenated nemesis. Every nuance of weather and change expressed their battle.

The Winter God stripped the trees and froze the earth, consuming the world's variety beneath blankets of snow, desiring a uniform world of cold and ice, valuing neither life nor colour. When the Sun God triumphed, he melted the snows, filled the trees, and grew food. He raised grass from softened ground and shone proudly over his work. The seasons predictably followed each other, the gods equally matched and neither capable of reigning without tiring. Time would never decide a winner; the world was forever tied to this inescapable routine.

He supported the Sun God unreservedly and hoped each summer the iridescent deity would deter the Winter God; but each time he was disappointed. When the days grew shorter and cold travelled in the winds, he knew the Sun God was beaten and his retreat had begun. The strength of these gods was demonstrated by the enormous changes they fashioned upon the world, but neither god approached the Wind God's power. The Wind God never tired or slept; he inhabited every recess under the sky, omnipresent without pause. He had witnessed the Wind God's greatest display of strength many seasons ago when first prying into adulthood.

Ten summers ago, his face still beardless, his family alive and loneliness unknown, the murderous winter was ending. The brutal season had mercilessly punished his group, killing nine and leaving eight. A single Moon cycle oversaw the death of his two youngest sisters, an infant cousin, every grandparent, an uncle, and an aunt. The eldest and youngest perished, leaving his parents, older brother, younger sister, uncle, cousin, and aunt.

Hunger had forced their travel. Their barren area had slowly starved them until desperation had evicted them from their winter caves to search for more generous lands. He remembered his tired grandmother staying behind, smilingly assuring him she would rest and catch up; he never saw her again. During the itinerant nights, the cold overran the fire's warmth, infecting the sleeping and vulnerable. The ravenous children and grandparents never woke from sleep, his famished aunt died in childbirth, and injury left his uncle behind.

The family postponed grief as they fought for survival. There was no time for mourning when death stalked so closely. They stoically persevered, acceptingly abandoning their dead to snowy graves, moving onwards, hunting an end to starvation.

Meagre scavenged foods rescued them while the Winter God weakened and began receding from the world. The depleted and despondent family were slowly encouraged by the withdrawing colds and dared to hope. He watched optimism and health gradually re-emerge in his family, growing his confidence that they would reach summer without suffering further loss.

Gradually the ice and snows melted, and heat trickled into the lengthening days, and the skies grew clear and blue, and the nights kind and hospitable. They wore less and ate more, slept later, and played often. They settled into a generous summer, rich with provisions and comfort. The family began nursing strength into their emaciated bodies and mending their damaged spirits. During these kinder days, they rediscovered contentment. The women grew pregnant again and the men less sullen, and slowly satiated expressions consumed gaunt faces.

His rehabilitation filled him with forgotten energy and his life regained the meaning it had lost inside the blizzards. Winter had relegated existence to struggle and stubborn perseverance through relentless storms. He had morosely trudged through the endlessly similar days, hopeless but obstinate, resisting surrender's temptations. But now purpose was reappearing and repossessing him of ambition and dreams. His body grew stronger and his muscles fuller, and the departing cold took with it his stress and pains. He playfully wrestled with the men again, enjoyed stories under starlight, and slept peacefully by fires wearing little. He felt his growing strength with pride.

At any opportunity he would measure himself by challenging his brother, striving to surmount the disability of being younger. Close age had ensured they were each other's principal companions, while time and shared responsibilities had made them inseparable and dependent. From his first steps he had followed his brother, and his parents had named him accordingly, Follows.

His older brother would happily accept his challenges and defeat him, invigorating Follows' efforts, and making competition their dynamic. His brother had been named Quiet during infancy for crying little, a behaviour following him into adulthood, never brash or loud.

When Follows was not hunting or competing with Quiet, his mind inadvertently wandered to women—a new pastime of increasing preoccupation. Without an outlet for his desires, his fancies and imaginings fell upon his aunt. She was new to the family; his uncle had stolen her two summers ago from another group. She had joined his uncle willingly, but his family had still been forced to flee the area to escape her family's reprisal.

At night, Follows imagined lying with her, possessing, and exploring her. He daydreamed of defending and winning her, defeating his uncle, and eloping with her. But his musings inevitably ended the same way, a return to reality and emptiness. Unable to realise his fantasies, and without an outlet for his affections, he became frustrated.

He kept his desires hidden, fearing his lusting would fracture their small group or earn him ridicule from the men. He knew as he grew his uncle would feel increasingly threatened, more suspicious of his coveting and protective of his partner. He understood these mistrusts could escalate into conflict and so confined his longings to unsatisfying dreams.

His female cousin had seen eight winters and would not partner for at least four more, but even then, his older brother had priority. He worried their family would never find another group, leaving him alone. The thought of never having a woman increasingly despaired and panicked him. It was these anxieties which provoked his long explorations into the wilderness looking for a partner.

His impatience and urges were not peculiar to him; Quiet was similarly afflicted. Unable to ignore their yearnings, they journeyed together, searching for signs of people. Their excursions probed their surroundings and guided them many horizons from camp. The impetus for their wanderings remained unspoken. Their conversations focused instead upon shared dreams, taking over groups, and defeating great animals; their debates probed existence, the afterlife, and the gods. They found opportunity to play often, inventing games and competitions to occupy their travels. He later reflected on these times as amongst his happiest.

Provided the brothers were not required for hunting or chores, the family allowed their explorations with understanding sympathy, keen to avoid fraying tempers. His father and uncle recognised the boys' motivations, but despite some amusement, they never trivialised their feelings. They realised the importance of acquiring a partner and knew lone males were more prone to impulsiveness, recklessness, violence, and reclusiveness.

His father appreciated the dangerousness of their wanderings but knew better than to constrain them. He knew significant disagreement during their impetuous ages could rupture their group and even kill. He would only intervene to preserve the group's solidity, never to forcibly assert his will and encourage challenge. So, he tolerated their searching, willing to assist if entreated.

Despite the brothers' searches, they never found trace of humans. Over the summer these frustrations sometimes cultivated irritation, causing occasional disagreements and rare separations. One day an argument over which direction to pursue precipitated their separation. Both riled by the other, they parted, neither brother wishing conflict with their closest companion, each understanding time and solitude placated moods.

Needing to expunge his annoyance, he walked faster and farther than on any previous day. He bounded under the falling sun, carving through long-grassed plains dyed in auburn evening light. He would have kept walking into the night if the world had not ended.

He was arrested by awe; his eyes widened, and his breath caught; his body seized and words disappeared. Before him lay a lake that stretched into forever, its brilliant blue filling every horizon. Uncertain moments followed, the alien scene was simultaneously alluring and disconcerting.

Gradually his caution lessened as the water's tranquillity calmed him. Overcome by his discovery's immensity, he sat upon its shimmering shore, staring at its glistening vastness, overwhelmed by its implications. He had found the world's edge and the boundary of creation. The scale of the gods' construction communicated his insignificance. He felt inconsequential beside such enormity, all his ambitions and undertakings suddenly trivial. He found new perspective and appreciated life's brevity and the gods' eternalness and power.

He knew no creature could ever cross these waters—it was a barrier as insurmountable as climbing the void between the ground and the sky. He had wondered before if the land was infinite, both along and below his feet. He had wondered whether he could walk forever without end, or if he dug deep enough, he would find a great emptiness. Now another of the world's mysteries was answered, deepening his understanding of existence.

The great truth of his world was its finiteness. Within the confines of this barricade resided finite lands, humans, and animals. He found this comforting, because an infinite world could never be mastered or fully explored, and now these prospects were not impossible.

He watched the lake, confused by its movement, rolling and crashing as if alive, wondering its purpose. He thought a long while before concluding it existed to stop the living from leaving the world and wandering into the immaterial where the gods had ceased creating.

His curiosity prompted him to approach the lake, his advance cautious to avoid any dangers. As he neared, the wind passed over him, carrying odours unlike any he had experienced. He paused to consider his safety and study his surroundings, trying to infer anything. He inspected the great lake and gradually reached an important realisation: the wind travelled into his world over these waters, creating the waves skating its surface.

He was unsure why the lake did not spill over existence's edge into nothingness, but he probed until he grasped the impressive truth. The Wind God lifted the lake from the void where creation ceased, his power relentless and inconceivable. He realised the Wind God existed everywhere and never tired. Through each season the Wind God watched over all creation, guarding night and day without reprieve. Even the great lake must have been built by the Wind God, for only he could sustain it. Such unparalleled strength was both stirring and intimidating.

Follows had never revered the Wind God but now realised his transgression. The Wind God was overseer of all life, guardian of the border separating the incorporeal and the material. Even the great Sun God tired and retreated behind the horizon each day to rest while the Wind God flowed throughout the world, witness and guide to everything without pause. Follows immediately respected such power, and knowing no greater protector and ally existed, he viscerally desired allegiance with such strength. Follows shouted his sentiments into the wind, remorseful he had not before recognised the Wind God's power.

'I know now you are the strongest god. You will always have my respect and veneration.'

The Wind God answered with light breezes, confirming he had heard him. Follows stood quietly, staring over the immense waters, finding it difficult to conclude company with such majesty. He remained until the darkening skies reminded him of his waiting family and persuaded him to return. But before he departed, he gathered his courage and neared the waves, curious to touch and taste the impregnable barrier. He knelt and sipped the strangely scented water and immediately grimaced at its brackishness. The lake's repulsive taste was designed to deter life from braving the waters, not to slake thirsts.

Follows looked at the great lake, simultaneously awed and saddened. He wanted to view the nothingness beyond the water, but knew such sights were impossible for his kind. He felt so powerless, his ability so constrained, yet his mind so boundless. The impassable lake made his life seem so constricted; he would never view nothingness or touch the stars, sit on clouds or visit godly lands.

He supposed the gods intended these feelings to enrich his spirit with revelation, inconsequentiality, and insight. He believed these profound moments connected him with the gods and exposed them to the human experiences their divinity disallowed. He hoped his insight endeared him to them and would earn his prayers more attention. He felt closer to his world and to understanding it, making him feel more sentient.

His thoughts were interrupted as the sun slowly crept towards the lake's horizon. Enthralled, he watched the sun descend into the lake, colouring the waters in incandescent brilliance. The beauty filled him with rapture and lifted him from mortal considerations. As the sun disappeared, the world slowly darkened and urged him to begin for home. He had witnessed a celestial display and experienced a revelation that made his life seem inconsequential; but cajoled by emerging hunger and shivered by the wind, he began towards home.

Before darkness seized the world, he settled amongst large rocks and prepared a fire, building some comfort within the stony edifice. The withdrawn sun let twilight fall upon the world and welcomed early stars upon the transitioning skies. He fell asleep watching the fire, relaxed and detached, reliving the day's discoveries. His eyes travelled within the flames until dreams replaced thought and the waking world faded.

When first light roused him, he returned to his relieved family. Their relief quickly dissolved into chastisement, but he bore the admonishment, knowing he deserved it. He disclosed nothing of his experience, feeling that verbalising the events would somehow dilute their profoundness and that human language could not explain his feelings. In his subsequent seasons, his silence preserved the experience's importance and prevented it being trivialised, allowing it to move him whenever recalled.

The succeeding seasons reunited him with the ocean, but these occasions were never as poignant. Nevertheless, the seas forever captivated him. After this event, he spoke often with the Wind God and felt his presence in each embracing wind. From then on, when starved of human interaction and conversation, he did not feel alone. He found consolation knowing his words and thoughts had an audience and were not lost inside the world, tempering the destructiveness of loneliness and lessening his despair.

Isolation prompted many discussions with the Wind God, and when undistracted, he felt the god's responses emerge in his mind. He reasoned the gods used such methods because lies could easily hide in human language, but not in thought. Such communication prohibited misunderstanding because feelings attached themselves to thoughts, allowing an openness and sincerity that language obscured.

When untroubled and without obligation, he sought explanations for his questions. The Wind God built answers in his mind, often using his own musings and speculations to ease his understanding.

'Do gods have form?' he asked the Wind God.

'We are shapeless. With form comes limitation, and we must be free from constraint to undertake boundless tasks. Could the Sun God look upon himself with mortal eyes, or lift himself with earthly hands? With form, my breath would not be infinite and could not keep the seas from existence's edge. And how would the Winter God ply his icy work throughout the world if form confined him to one place?'

'Why do you care what happens in the world?'

'Your body is only temporary, but your wisdom journeys with your spirit. The world is your teacher, that is why the gods created it. You must understand the emotions that only man and animal can experience, whether it is fear, lust, anger, or joy. Knowing these feelings will provide you with the wisdom to understand the living when you have left the world.'

'Does a spirit feel differently to man?'

'When you sit and feel at peace, when your concerns have temporarily lifted, when you're free from drive and ambition, when the world is quiet and beautiful, then your spirit is freed from mortal concerns. The spirit does not desire anything, for nothing tangible has use. It is content—without hunger, fear, pain, or suffering. The alleviation of worldly struggle is the reward for enduring your difficult life. Living is a task we must all undertake to broaden our spirit's eternal perspective.'

Follows often restrained his questioning, careful to avoid exhausting the Wind God's patience so he could preserve their friendship. He believed the clarity of the Wind God's responses usually indicated the subject's secrecy, for sometimes his mind was flooded with responses and other times nothingness. When unsatisfactory answers arose, he wondered if divine secrets were being kept from him. Sometimes conversations only inspired more questions and confusion, riddling his subsequent days with wild conjecture. He always felt close to discovering a great truth about existence but reckoned the limits of human intelligence held him from revelation. Eventually and inexorably his interest waned, and survival would reoccupy him.

After Quiet's death, the Wind God had become his closest friend, helping to distract him from loneliness and grief, regrowing his confidence and reinstilling self-worth. He told the Wind God about his plans and the life he hoped for. Somewhere, seasons hence, the Settlement waited, hidden by countless horizons and buried deep inside the world. His journey was long and dangerous, and he needed his god's protection.

Sometimes he spoke of women, hoping the Wind God would aid his search for a partner and help end his loneliness.

THREE

THE GROWING WARMTH OF the days and nights had tempted him into believing the blizzards had retreated until next winter. But despite the heavens' promises, another storm came.

Dark skies had swiftly gathered, leaving him insufficient time to find shelter. He watched desperately as the storm fell upon the world, consuming light and heat, concealing the distance. His escape had forced him to travel without seeking shelters, leaving no refuge behind him within reach, and his only chance of survival lay in the unknown land ahead. He hated himself for planning so inadequately, and he cursed both his imprudence and winter's misdirection, furious he might die so abjectly.

Thick snow and fog cloaked the surroundings, leaving him at the tempest's mercy. Engulfed in the storm he was blind, fuelling his panic. Clad in his every fur, he violently thrashed through the torrents, desperately fighting the Winter God's death throes, searching frantically for shelter.

Cold lashed his face and the winter wind speared through his furs, causing every part of him to shake. He fought onwards but no cover emerged from the storm, leaving him defenceless. The snowstorm escalated into a blizzard, and the snow underfoot began burying each step, sapping his speed and demanding increasing exertion. He was dragged close to standstill, every stride laboured and deep. From a lone tree, he collected small pine branches and, with failing fingers, tied them to his feet, partially moderating his submersion.

His arms held to his chest, he resisted the urge to bury his head down, needing to keep his eyes up and searching. His hands and feet lost feeling, so he quickened his pace to warm them. He realised such exertion was unsustainable and that he would collapse into exhaustion sooner, but the conditions disallowed him choice.

He knew that failure to find shelter would leave him exposed, drained, and prey to death. He had seen extreme cold's madness infect people, slowly stealing their senses and finally their consciousness. He had witnessed people attempt sleep and undress as cold insanity possessed them. During these ordeals, he had noticed his own diminishing awareness but stubbornly intensified his efforts to survive. He understood cold's debilitation—he would not let winter kill him without vicious resistance.

He fought the storm, his senses blurring and faculties deteriorating. But then, through fading awareness, he noticed vague, black forms emerge from the shrouded distance. The dark silhouettes encouraged him forward and, slowly, snow-capped rocks surfaced. His straining legs trudged amongst the rubble, searching for the rock that had birthed them. Fear overpowered his degrading alertness and propelled him amongst the debris.

A cliff rose from hiding and he raced to it. His numb hands fell upon its walls, imploring it to yield him shelter. The temptation to cower into the rock and escape the wind was seducing, but he collected himself, needing to investigate his discovery for better cover.

He scoured the rock wall, exposed but persevering, searching for any cavity that could rescue him. Bare trees patrolled the cliff, sporadic and useless. The wind besieged him pitilessly, stifling his efforts and diminishing his clarity. His desperation grew more maniacal and violent, and he tore around the rockface, terrified and wild. Suddenly, heaped boulders stopped him, presumably a recent landslide. His hope rallied; he knew cavities within the rocks could protect him until the blizzard passed.

He explored amongst the rocks, unbalanced by shivering and limbs slowing, until he found a small passageway at the base of two enormous rocks. He dived into it and wriggled along its gravel floor until he emerged into an open space. He raised himself inside the rockfall's enclosed darkness and probed it with outstretched hands. Its width was three paces and its depth uneven and boulder littered. The ground was covered with stone shards, but dry. Scant gaps decorated the ceiling and floor, but they were small.

He exhaled, relieved; he could outwait the storm here. But he needed fire—he was shaking, dreary, and dead without heat. He dropped his pack and spear and returned outside, where he beat through the colourless day to the bare trees. He made two laden journeys to collect enough firewood to survive the night.

When he returned, he began his fire, shaking and tense. His unsteady hands impeded him, but eventually the tinder ignited, and the flame flourished. As the fire thrived, he wrung the water from his hair, then undressed and placed his soaked furs beside the heat. The smoke escaped through the ceiling's openings, drawn outwards by passing winds. The fire threw light into the enclosure's depths, illuminating its rocky corridor fifteen paces deep, crowded by boulders and stone shards. The hearth's warmth slowly rehabilitated his mood and stilled his chattering teeth. His anxiety gradually melted, allowing his exhaustion.

He sat against the enclosure's wall, his breathing slowing as his tension faded. His mind drifted to his previous winter shelter and its mounds of hides, its painted walls decorated with his stories, and his frozen meats preserved in snow. During winter's most vicious days and nights, he had nestled within heaped furs, beside benevolent fires, safe from the frost and cold outside. The memory of his winter cave and its warm boredom now seemed a paradise compared to his current predicament.

But he also recalled the restlessness which had expedited his departure: his struggle with confinement and the difficulty of life alone without much stimulation or novelty. His impatience and unchanelled energy had encouraged him to abandon his shelter early, and desperate to escape imprisonment's frustrations, he had acquiesced.

His thoughts were carrying him towards sleep, but he pulled himself awake, needing to dress and feed the fire, aware of the danger of collapsing without these protections. While he dressed and warmed, his hunger worsened. He ate his few remaining foods, but they did not satisfy him, so he accepted hunger until the storm lifted.

He stacked more wood upon the fire, judging it had dried enough to house flame. But as the fire caught the wood, an almost imperceptible rustle resonated from the cave's depths. He was not alone. He was immediately alert but suppressed reaction, mindful to avoid startling or unnerving whatever lurked nearby. Hiding his fright, he mentally readied for response.

Whatever creature lay hidden within the twisting passage could not be larger than him—the entranceway had barely permitted his entry—so he decided against escape. He briefly shifted his eyes to his spear, habitually kept within reach, reassured by its closeness. He wondered if this creature was sleeping, explaining its hitherto silence. Regardless, he gained the advantage by attacking, which committed him to action.

His hand crept towards his spear, his motions calm and soundless, his eyes looking elsewhere to hide his intentions. His fingers found the spear and folded around it. He pulled his knees to his chest, positioning himself to launch forwards. His chest thumped and he forgot his exhaustion. His free hand fell towards the fire and clasped a branch ablaze with flame. He summoned his violence, preparing for conflict and its required brutality.

Then he flung the branch into the enclosure's darkness and leapt to his feet, spear raised ready to throw. The burning wood fell amongst the gloom and illuminated the cave's depths. A black shape shifted and lurched towards the back wall, aware of its discovery and his danger. Without hesitation, he hurled his spear towards the shape, but the layered shadows upset his aim and the spear tore into the rearmost wall, narrowly missing. The creature immediately cowered behind a rock.

A panting and alarmed creature peered from behind the boulder, its face and identity revealed by the flame. It was a human, ensuring him a vicious confrontation. He stiffened for conflict and readied for its charge, but no attack came. He held the gaze examining him, fire dancing in its eyes, full of fear and begging mercy, its stooped body poised to leap should he advance.

During these tense moments, his eyes wandered over the person's outline, trying to discover anything of his company. But his mind stumbled, the shape confusing, forbidding him any conclusions—the prominent muscle indicated a male, but the shape and features were female, prohibiting him from responding appropriately.

He pulled another burning branch from the fire and pitched it near the recoiling figure, chasing away more darkness. Long red hair and a large flat nose emerged from the dark. A heavy protruding brow sat over frightened eyes, and the forehead receded towards a low hairline. It was female, but it was not a woman. There was too much muscle and foreignness; it was a Neanderthal female.

She had seen about twenty winters, her appearance alien, fascinating, and disconcerting. He was neither attracted nor repulsed, noticing only the creature's fear, strangeness, and desperation to escape. She presented little danger, and in different circumstances he might have attempted communication, but pragmatism decided his response.

He could not sleep in her company and chance her mercy;

neither could he expel her into the blizzard. If she found her group, she could vengefully return, leaving him trapped and outnumbered. His attack would have stoked her indignation and would encourage her to protect herself by killing him. Soon he would collapse into sleep, providing her an opportunity to exploit his vulnerability; but he would not chance that.

The solution was inescapable, but it still provoked a sombre reluctance. She was not threatening him and desired clemency. Yet the situation had decided her fate. Reluctant to kill the female with his hands, he backed towards his second spear, holding her distressed stare as he progressed towards her.

But she recognised his intention and impulsively flung herself upon him, seizing him without plan or maliciousness. Reflexively, he seized her wrists and held her, his strength frightening her immobile. A hand's length separated their fastened eyes, each inspecting an alien face, hers etched with distress. Quiet moments of indecision passed without malice, aggression, or understanding.

The female's expressions seemed so recognisably human, but she was not human, and he struggled free from empathy. She was no physical equal, but he felt her strength: a strength superior to human women that hardened his resolve to kill her.

He forced her to the ground, his stare threatening violence should she resist. She fell to the gravel floor, wearing terror and desperation. Her anguish pleaded mercy, but he suppressed sympathy. With locked eyes, he moved towards his second spear, watching her stillness, wondering if it was fear that caused her inaction, or the hope that he would be merciful. He saw her distress climb as he seized his spear, and she realised her fate.

He moved too quickly to allow her any defence. In a moment, his spear had left his hand, exploded through her sternum, and surfaced through her back. A moroseness consumed the cave and held him captive to her ugly end.

Paralysed disbelief gripped the Neanderthal. Her hands rose

to her wound, reflexively covering the injury as she choked. Her blinking eyes locked with his, her eyelids flickered, her face frozen with shock. Then she lurched, twisting in agony, eyes searching for some impossible release from the pain.

He had fought and killed many men before but never felt regret, just deep relief. Confrontations never allowed him sympathy for his opponents, his survival had always justified their deaths. But now he watched discomposed as the Neanderthal gagged and bled. Finally, she collapsed against the rock wall, dead eyes staring at nothingness, blood pooling beneath her.

He sighed, shaken by her dying, but felt the beginnings of some relief. Her eyes were divested of accusation and no longer condemning. Tension left his body, readiness unnecessary and sleep tonight safe. Now dead, justifying her killing was easier. The gods would understand his conduct; man's minds were theirs to read.

He tiredly considered the twisted body. He could not remove her outside and chance her kin happening upon her and inviting their revenge. He had to accept her company until the weather improved and allowed his escape.

His exhaustion began reasserting itself, defeating his concerns and demanding he rest. He crossed the enclosure and collapsed beside the fire. He fed its flames and reclined into warmth. Ignoring his hunger, he dissolved into sleep.

Inside the cave's stillness, time turned the fire into cinders and ash, and the warmth that had allowed him to rest escaped into the storm. Outside, the snow thrashed upon the world and winds whistled by, stealing his heat until the cold woke him.

He woke groggy, hungry, thirsty, and cold. He looked through the ceiling's gaps but saw only snow and mist. Needing to replenish his firewood, he rose and entered the blizzard. He moved carefully through the storm, looking for signs of other Neanderthals but seeing nothing. When returned inside, he restored the fire and laid wood around it. He melted fresh snow and drank until satisfied.

Feeling better, he relaxed against the rock wall, eyes resting closed, tired thoughts drifting.

He thought about the female and the first time he had encountered a Neanderthal. He had seen only seven winters back then, but the memory felt recent and clear. His mother had taught him about the Neanderthal's accidental creation, and the war between Neanderthal and man. They were a cursed species; rejected by the gods and left to wander without purpose or guidance.

> *The cloudless blue winter sky reached into each horizon. The cold heavens overlooked the fur-wrapped brothers carving their father's kill, alone, talkative, and jovial. The men were hunting abroad, the women were shaping clothes at their camp half a horizon away.*
>
> *Follows and Quiet were stripping the deer and periodically returning its meat to camp. They casually performed their charge with both practised experience and the boredom of familiar routine. With only conversation and the company of evergreens, each worked quickly. The habitual practice created an ordinariness that made the subsequent event more disquieting.*
>
> *The day's tranquillity was shattered. From snow-laden trees burst a violent struggle between two entangled adversaries. The commotion raised the boys to standing, ready to run. Yet astonishment overpowered them and held them captive.*
>
> *A foreign man, abnormally broad, muscular, and squat, was locked in conflict with a bull reindeer. The man's body communicated immense physical strength, a capacity he powerfully exerted over the thrashing buck. A snapped wooden shaft protruded*

from the deer's neck, spilling trails of dark blood over virgin snows. The foreign man held the buck's antlers, ferociously trying to wrestle it to the ground. The bull divided its response between writhing attempts to wrest free and thrusting efforts to impale.

Fascination paralysed the brothers; the inhuman strength was enthralling. Curious to witness the extraordinary confrontation's outcome, they remained, noticing the bull lose the advantage when charging. Had it concentrated on extricating itself, it would have succeeded—each twisting retreat forced the man to cling on helplessly. But when the deer thrust forward, the man drove it into the ground, almost upending it.

Finally, the man overturned the deer and crashed it into the snow, then leapt behind it and wrapped himself around its neck. The deer violently flailed and kicked, furiously trying to reacquire control. The foreign man reached for the wooden shaft and pulled it from the deer. Undeterred by the death throes crushing him the man drove the bloody weapon repeatedly into the deer. The deer's struggle gradually abated as it surrendered consciousness and collapsed. The foreign man disentangled himself from the animal and stood, heavily lacerated but composed.

Only when the foreign man stood alone did the brothers fully appreciate his strangeness. His shoulders were abnormally wide and his enormous chest round. His legs were thick and short, his muscle pronounced, his skin pale, his nose flat, his hair red. The freakish man drastically contrasted their father's lithe and nimble body, his strength inferably superior but his agility less.

The strange man fixed the boys with deep-set green eyes, his stare uncertain and questioning. It took only a moment before fear broke the brothers' transfixion and instinctive flight overtook them. The two boys fled for camp, leaving the strange man staring after them, alone with his kill, panting heavily into the winter air.

When Follows reflected on that day in the subsequent seasons, he remembered no malice in the alien features, only indecisiveness and unease. The encounter would haunt him, partly for exposing his own inadequate strength, but mostly because time never helped him understand the worried green eyes.

The brothers burst into camp, calling to the women, concurrently recounting the incident. When the boys finished their account, worry overtook the women. They debated their response: whether to shift camp and leave the men to track them, or remain and wait for the men to return.

Eventually they decided against leaving. Moving would confuse the returning men, and if darkness hid their tracks, they would be left unprotected until dawn. So they waited, fireless, ears trained on the surroundings, listening for the unusual. As they waited, the boys huddled with their mother under furs, eyes trailing the dark.

'What was that man, Mother?' Quiet murmured.

In whispers their mother told them of the Neanderthal: the creature the boys had witnessed.

'They are a cursed species, their perverted form born from two amalgamated creatures. They are lost without purpose in a world not made for them, without identity or the gods' love.'

'Why do the gods not care for them?' Follows whispered.

Their mother leant closer, keeping her voice low.

'Hundreds of winters ago, man grew jealous of the speed, strength, and fur of other animals. They quarrelled with the gods over their vulnerability, protesting that without the hides of animals, they died, without a group they were killed, and without fire they froze.

'Finally, the gods proposed a compromise. They offered man the strength of bears and their imperviousness to cold, but insisted that in exchange man relinquish human resourcefulness, his ability to throw spears, and human beauty—for gods rewarded man with beauty for bearing their harsh lives. The gods would not allow any animal significant advantage over others, for they wished to maintain the balance that allowed all creatures to coexist. The gods thought these conditions would deter people from choosing to change themselves, but blinded by their suffering and gluttonous for strength, some humans abandoned sense and chose to change.

'And so, the gods split man into two creatures. Many remained human, but many became the Changed Man. The Changed Man initially revelled in his new abilities, chasing down prey without weapons and wandering comfortably through the harshest winters. But despite these freedoms the Changed Man still lusted for human beauty.

'Finally, desperate yearning caused the Changed Man to raid human camps. Without throwing weapons, some were killed, but their superior strength won them victory. Human men and women were torn from their families and ravaged to satisfy *irrepressible desires. But when the gods saw these acts, they damned their creation and vengefully cast lightning upon each changed person, destroying the species forever. But the Changed Man's depravity bred a new species. Human women conceived during the raid, breeding a mixed creature—the Neanderthal. The human women bore no compassion for these infants, nor would any community accept the children because of their forebears' attack.*

'The humans evicted the Neanderthals, unwilling to cohabit with this product of their violation. The gods did not destroy the creature—it was not guilty of any crime—but neither could they understand nor guide the beast, for they had not designed it. Its duality was incomprehensible and its divided mind unreasonable, so the gods abandoned it without supervision and direction amongst accepted creatures.

'The Neanderthal's expulsion made them despise humans. They wanted revenge for their abandonment and purposelessness, and sought war with man. There has been conflict ever since. Though our kind must bear this violent rivalry, our fight is just. Each felled Neanderthal brings the world closer to being free of its unnatural kind.'

Their mother finished, leaving the brothers awed and silent. Neither boy spoke, lost in the story.

They waited tensely until the men finally returned. There were no fires that night. The men remained awake, guarding, watching the darkness and patrolling to lessen the chance of ambush. In the morning their group moved far away, nobody willing to chance the creature's intentions. He had seen no Neanderthal since.

But the Neanderthal did become a brutal and strong antagonist in the brothers' games. Yet these games inevitably ended the same way. Human cunning usually defeated the Neanderthal's physical advantage, its downfall accelerated by its inescapable wildness.

He realised these games had distorted the Neanderthal and created an animal unlike the male and female Neanderthals he had encountered. The gulf between the story and memory was discomforting, but he knew his duty to his own species. The war with the Neanderthal had demanded his involvement—for the protection of his species was the protection of his descendants—and he had acted dutifully. Her death was only a fragment of an ancient conflict he had not started nor would finish. He could be proud of eliminating an unnatural creature and making the world safer for man. And though she was no direct danger to humans, she could birth males that threatened his kind—threats he had prevented. He would not burden himself by further questioning his actions; he let his mind empty and drift away. He fell back into sleep and left the fire to burn away.

When he woke, he felt rested, but his hunger was awful. Outside, the same white mist stared back, making the duration of his stay indeterminable, though he suspected a night and a day.

His hunger began provoking his irritation. He turned to the Neanderthal, stiffened and pale, her decay delayed by cold. He suddenly wondered why he had not eaten her. He supposed tiredness had damaged his sense, or unconsciously attaching humanity to her; but now he saw his oversight and eagerly seized upon her.

He stripped and cooked some meat and urgently ate. The food immediately lessened his stress, his shoulders relaxed, and his temper calmed. He retrieved snow from outside and buried the remaining meat for later. He struggled to recognise the humanity he had earlier perceived and found his prior sympathies difficult to recall. He saw only food as her impression faded, making his former feelings seem absurd and irrational.

Follows ate sparingly over the next two days, exercising restraint lest the storm outlast his food. But moderation was unnecessary—the storm faded first. When light breached the enclosure's gaps, he rose and looked outside. A pale-blue sky peered through breaks in the cloud; snowflakes still fell, but the storm had retired.

He needed to distance himself quickly; the female's family would be searching for her. Follows packed the remaining meat, collected up his possessions, and fled outside into light snowfall and intermittent sunshine.

Within four horizons the snow had ceased, and the skies were clear. Weak sunlight touched his face, and the distance shed its mist. Icy winds still beat against his back but soon even the cold would fade. The Winter God's final offensive was defeated, and the Sun God had emerged exhausted but triumphant, the world his to paint.

His travel lifted his mood and separated him from restlessness, reinvigorating his mind and energies. His thoughts returned to the Neanderthal, remembering her frightened eyes and fitful dying. The memory was sobering, but he felt no guilt—duty and practicality had killed her. Instead he was saddened by her existence; born without choice into conflict but wanting peace, like prey born to be hunted. Even her desire for children conflicted with his existence. He supposed all life defied the world's intimidations and bore young despite the hardships that awaited them.

He pushed the Neanderthal from his mind; he was alive, nothing was more important. He could continue towards the Settlement, find its munificent lands and people, end his lonely existence, and build a family. He would allow nothing chance to endanger these dreams.

He strode on, possessed by obsession and hope. The dying winter held him inside its faltering clasp, its gales and storms conceding defeat until rested.

FOUR

THE STORM HAD BEEN winter's last. Since the blizzard, the days had grown longer and warmer; the snows had softened and then disappeared. He walked barefoot through newly green grasses, naked against the sun. The Sun God shone proudly against blue skies, nurturing the blossoming world below.

Some retained furs remained, tied and bound to his pack, saved only for nocturnal comfort and summer rains. The morning dew pleasantly soaked his feet, welcome against his hard skin. The grass underfoot was soft and each step comfortable.

He moved across a ridgeline overlooking vast grasslands. His silhouette carved clear against the sky, but his vantage point afforded him forewarning's protection, allowing him to drift peacefully but safely. His eyes wandered the sun-bathed world, searching without urgency for water to satisfy his thirst.

After a time, he saw a small brook and approached to drink. Moving waters were safe, as spirits only bathed in stagnant waters and imbibing them could lead to sickness. He drank until refreshed, then stood, eyes following the brook until it joined a lake. He walked towards it, noticing deer upon its opposite shore, but he had no hunting intentions. Surrounding the lake soared newly flush deciduous trees, their winter skeletons buried beneath new green.

The deer noticed his approach but disregarded him. He welcomed the deer's indifference, pleased that they remained, preferring to keep their company over solitude, and impressed they recognised his peacefulness. He resolved to return their tolerance with deference and quiet.

He sat upon the lake's bank, removed his pack, and nestled into the soft grass. The surroundings encouraged calm, slowing his breathing and stealing his impetus. But rest was not his intention, he sought the spirits' counsel and knew they drank at still waters on hot days.

Many summers ago, his father had proven the spirits' existence and taught him where to seek their counsel. To reveal the spirits, his father had placed a bowl of water underneath the midday sun.

'Spirits will drink this water,' his father had told him. 'Look over the bowl and you will see the air distort. This warped air is water being drawn into their formless bodies. On hot days this phenomenon lets you know spirits are present. If you need to ask their advice, or for protection, then seek still waters on hot days.'

By evening, his father's claims were proven: the bowl had emptied. He remembered his astonishment with both nostalgia and sadness, sorry that his father was gone.

The spirits' counsel had steered him to the lake; he needed to assuage his uncertainty about the Settlement. He reclined into the hill rising from the shore, eyes wandering the water, watching the air distort. Rippled air traversed the entire lake, assuring him many spirits were present and that his question would be heard and perhaps answered.

'I am following the stars towards a divine group,' he murmured, careful not to upset the surrounding calm. 'Generations ago, a god left the heavens to love a woman, endowing their descendants with divine insight. Their lineage created and still leads the Settlement, a group of over five hundred. In this place, people never starve, cold doesn't kill, people live to impossible ages, every newborn grows to adulthood, and people do not kill for partners or standing.

'I've travelled two summers hoping the Settlement will end my loneliness and hardship, but sometimes I suspect it too fantastical to exist. I ignore these doubts, believing the gods are steering me, but my uncertainty persists. I don't ask assistance or protection, only a sign that my travel is not misguided.'

Follows finished, hopeful of a response. He was without urgency and happy to wait. Most spirits would be uninterested in assisting him—man's material concerns were of little interest—but he only needed one to help.

He looked over his surroundings, eyelids heavy under the heat. His attention meandered to the deer, their restfulness soothing. He felt his breathing slow and deepen, each exhale pleasant and warm. He slackened into the grass, remembering how he had felt similarly after long days with his brother. They would settle in the evening, sharing tiredness, quiet with their own thoughts, watching the changing sky until the light faded and cold swept away warmth. During these moments, he most appreciated the gods' art and power and the beauty they could create. Their creation made him simultaneously realise his insignificance and most appreciate being alive.

These memories moved him. He knew such feelings were fragile and that tasks would soon bury them, but these rare moments left him desiring nothing but the present and let him feel fulfilled. This calm was so uncommon that he realised the spirits must be responsible.

The spirits had heard his request and delivered him this sign. His calm, and the memories of his brother, had been provoked to show him contentment was still possible, and that worry about his travel was unnecessary. The Settlement's existence was confirmed; he could discard his doubts.

He lay in the grass and closed his eyes; his journey could wait. He reflected on the spirits' subtlety and man's limits, impressed by the spirits' ways and language, and disappointed such was beyond him. He felt sure an end to loneliness and a new beginning was closer. Soon he might even find someone to care for, and perhaps someone to care for him.

Quiet had been his last family, and his death had left him completely alone. Follows remembered Quiet's death and his own subsequent collapse. But the gods had intervened to save him, and the Settlement had given him purpose amongst his despair.

Two summers ago, dawn light spilled into the night, pouring colour onto the early world. Two brothers emerged from the shadows: one fevered and near death, the other traumatised and cradling him. Their furs were blood matted, faces drawn and exhausted. Burnt spearheads lay beside them—one brother's shoulder was punctured, cauterised, and rotten; he would die that morning, and the remaining brother would be without any family for the first time.

Follows held Quiet, staring into vacated eyes where his brother had once been. He did not know how to be alone. He had never been a day without his sibling; even his name had been born from their relationship.

Before Quiet died, hunters from their group found them. The men asked Follows what had happened, but he was too broken to respond. Instead, they found signs of a recent auroch stampede and concluded it had caused his brother's injury. The hunters fetched medicine, furs, food, and water; but after doing what they could, keeping company with Follows and his grief proved difficult, and they left the brothers to conclude their relationship.

As Follows willed his connection to his past to survive, Quiet died. The world was still. Reality seemed suddenly insubstantial and distant. His mind felt disconnected, his thoughts incoherent dreams. Neither hunger nor cold could be felt; past and future disappeared, only uncomfortable moments existed. Finally, a bitterness emerged, at the world, the gods, and existence.

For most of their lives, the brothers had been each other's only company. In childhood, their group had been just their family, which winters and starvation had kept few. When a raid orphaned them in boyhood, they had fended alone, obstinate against hunger, predators, weather, and violence. It was only in adulthood that they had found a group to live amongst.

The brothers had joined this group to acquire the family and protection they had grown without, but despite investing themselves, they had never found acceptance. Without familial ties and shared history, they were always regarded as outsiders. They remained each other's chief company, never growing close with others. Patiently they had strived for acceptance, believing integration possible once partnered with the group's daughters, but when his brother stopped breathing, these hopes and all meaning died.

When Follows finally left his brother's body, he did not return to the group; instead he slumped inside a forest to avoid people's empty condolences. Alone, he drifted through memories of his brother, each recollection a harrowing reminder of his loss. Uninterested in anything, emptied of drive and spirit, he fell increasingly apart.

He watched pine branches swaying in the summer breeze, following the sunbeams moving between their shifting canopy gaps, his thoughts self-destructive and morbid. From somewhere inside his abyss, he had hoped the forest's quiet would lessen his grief; but it persisted without diminishment. His pain spilled out in choked words, hopeful that some essence of his brother would hear him and somehow return to him.

He lay there until the day grew old and the light thin, hoping for sleep and its release, until the quiet was interrupted by the voices of returning hunters. Their conversation began distant and indistinct, but as they neared, he heard his brother being discussed. He recognised the voice: a senior man in their group. He tried ignoring the men, but when he heard the senior man express relief that his brother was dead, Follows' loathing erupted, sanity left him, and self-control was impossible. Without plan, he leapt up and burst through the trees, intoxicated with violence.

Despite being startled, the hunters rallied to restrain Follows before he could unleash his hatred. They seized and held Follows while he screamed at the senior man, challenging him to fight, wildly damning him with every hate saturated curse he could muster.

The men dragged Follows away while the senior man watched, outwardly unmoved but internally seething. Grief was no excuse. He had been disrespected by an inferior in front of his men, riling him beyond forgiveness. He needed to fight and kill Follows to extinguish his threat and to make an example of him.

The senior male was older, stronger, and heavier, and emboldened by these advantages, he ordered his remaining hunters to inform their group of the insult and assemble them for the fight. Men attempted to dissuade the senior man—aware of Follows' dangerousness—but he would not relent, defensive of his reputation and wary of cohabiting with such hatred.

When the group had gathered, Follows was released. He marched to their camp and the senior man, his hate insatiable, consequence irrelevant. At the camp an audience had gathered: silent, nervous, and excited. He walked past them to the senior man, who stood waiting, eager to kill him. But the senior man was immediately overpowered, and became the victim of passionate cruelty delivered without leniency. The ruthlessness paralysed the audience with fear, unable to intervene.

When Follows' mania finally lifted, the senior man lay dead, disfigured, and eviscerated. Follows raised himself and walked away, without comment or interaction, glazed eyes turned towards the wilderness, blood coated, his footsteps staining a trail. He stumbled towards the river to clean himself, aware he would now have to leave the group. Some men would eventually rescue their nerve and seek revenge; yet concern was difficult. He was unsure of where to go, and unable to imagine living without his brother to share his experiences and have his affection and interdependency lend him value.

Follows climbed into the river and fell to his knees, without urgency to escape, spiritless and drained. He feebly washed away the blood, mounted the bank, and sat upon the shore. He watched the water traipse its stony bed as the fading sun dried him. He listlessly attempted to resurrect drive, until he noticed an approaching unarmed man. The approach seemed peaceful so Follows waited. He recognised the man, one of the few he had liked; a quiet old man that never made him feel like an outsider.

Follows was impassive as the old man stopped three paces from him. He looked up at the old man—his long grey hair braided and tied, his body thin and sinewy, his skin tanned and weathered. In his old eyes, Follows saw no malice or violence, just thoughtfulness, neither judging nor forgiving. They remained silent, each waiting for the other to speak.

They had never been close friends, but through hunting together they had grown trust and respect. The old man had joined the group as a child, grown with it, partnered with a girl, fathered four surviving children, and was grandfather to three. The old man had demonstrated to the brothers that integration was possible and been the example they had aspired to.

Finally, impatient from waiting, Follows spoke.

'Why are you here?' he asked.

'They will kill you, Follows,' the old man told him. 'You must leave.'

A silence followed. He knew the old man was right, but survival and life currently held little appeal. He turned his eyes to the horizon and the disappearing sun, trying to end the conversation. The old man watched Follows—young, heavily scarred, tall, lean, alone, distraught, and lost. The old man pitied him.

'I originally came from a distant group led by a divine child,' the old man continued. 'Here people *did not kill for partners, influence, survival, food, or shelter. There is abundant food, so hunger is unknown, even in winter. The group never moves and so constructs elaborate shelters for each resident, providing everyone safety and comfort in every season. Abundance lets people live to impossible ages without burdening the young. This Settlement can give you a new life.'*

Despite his dejection, the story was intriguing. Follows disguised his interest and scrutinised the story, hesitant to involve himself, acquainted with hope and its often-deceitful misdirection. Projecting indifference, he questioned the old man.

'If such a place exists, why did your family leave?'

'My parents died before I was old enough to question their reasons. Conjecture is rarely useful, but my parents joined the Settlement after a lifetime of nomadism, and perhaps permanently settling was difficult for them. But their reasons are irrelevant. You have nothing here except vengeful company. The Settlement is a future, I can give you its whereabouts, it was my only inheritance. You have the legs to get there, you need only the will to move them.'

Hesitant, but seeing a chance to live again, Follows met the old man's gaze and nodded. The old man returned the gesture, pleased.

'Follow the river downstream and wait in cover, I'll meet you at twilight. I'll bring you food, clothes, and spears, and give you the stars and directions to follow.'

Then the old man left for camp, knowing further encouragement was unnecessary.

That night they met downriver, amongst the trees lining the waterway. The heavens were fortunately clear of cloud and ignited by the early Moon and stars. When the old man gave him the promised items, Follows succumbed to the gratefulness he naturally found difficult. Then they discussed the route and the stars to follow, the group of over five hundred people, and the God Chief. But finally, Follows' restlessness to begin the journey ended their exchange.

He thanked the old man and left, without looking back or further questioning his undertaking. It took only a few steps before he felt some small deliverance. He had a future to distance him from the past, and an opportunity to leave behind ugly memories and the unwanted parts of himself. Perhaps in time he would mend; perhaps the Settlement could fulfil his and his brother's ambitions.

Darkness held him as colour left the skies, the night winds chased away summer's warmth, and his group disappeared behind. He followed the shifting starlight through the night, fleeing the horror of his brother's death.

FIVE

THE SUMMER DAYS TOOK him far from the lake. The long days melted into temperate nights and allowed him to walk into starlight painted darkness until tiredness turned into rest. At night he settled under star strewn skies, comfortable and satisfied with his progress. Each summer day covered the distance of ten midwinter days, each sunset a reminder he was closer. Uninhibited by worry, his mind wandered, provoking frequent conversations with the gods. He traipsed through dusk still in discussion, feeling accepted and protected by divine company.

Around a hundred and fifty days since leaving the lake, he settled into long grass outside a forest, underneath clear night sky. The dark celestial emptiness lay covered in white starlight and streaked by dust. The crescent-shaped Moon hung proudly, luminescent, like a campfire in twilight. Each night, the Moon climbed the night sky to show the world her pregnancy. She was mother to all the gods, and her lover, the Night God, the father. As her pregnancy developed, she grew and shone brighter, joyous with expectancy.

After the First God created the universe, and before the world, before form and shape, there had been just the night sky. But the First God's touch brought the Night God into existence, where he lived tranquilly alone inside his endless emptiness, unknowing of anything besides darkness, ignorant of the potential of his universe. But although he knew nothing except the night, the infinite time alone caused a loneliness that stole contentment.

The Night God knew only dark and so created a companion that would fill his sky with its opposite. He toiled an incomprehensible time, but finally the Moon was born, and she rose to scatter light upon his dark. He loved her instantly, his serene life made more beautiful, and his loneliness forgotten in affection.

The two gods became forever inseparable, leading inevitably to offspring. Each birth became a star, a powerless and delicate infant. As the stars grew, they became gods, inheriting new abilities and slowly enriching the universe with life and matter, creating new forms and phenomena. The passion of the universe's parents never waned, and each night the Moon rejoined her partner to display her love and pregnancy, and so would the universe always grow richer.

From his hill, his head cushioned by furs, Follows watched the night sky, comfortable and tired. He draped another fur over his legs, content to fall asleep under the Moon. The thousands of stars crossed above, their constellations and positions telling their histories. When young, he had sat around campfires listening to the adults' stories about the stars. Their positions had been shaped by wars, alliances, loves, banishments, and allegiances. He could recount the story of each cluster and prominent star, each a memory of its campfire regaling long ago.

He was grateful for the legends, and unsure how he could have known the night sky's secrets without them. He knew each trial, triumph, and pain of the young gods, their existences illustrated warnings and guidance for every observer. During his loneliest seasons, he had watched the stars united by love, fascinated but envious of their unions, aching to experience their companionship.

He hoped one day to sit around campfires with his own children, their attentions fastened to the same stories. In a thousand generations, he hoped his descendants would tell the same stories to their children, their lives his legacy. He wondered whether these distant descendants would bear resemblance to him as his brother had to their father. He remembered his father explaining inherited similarity.

> *'A child is the marriage of a couple's spirits. The gods create life from the essence of the mother and father, reassembling their pieces to form a new person. It is why families exhibit likenesses, and outsiders none. We instinctively protect our family to safeguard our shared spirit. The infant is shaped by the parts of each parent, whether the parts are strong or weak. Most children die before knowing adulthood because only the strongest combinations of each parent will survive. The gods created a harsh world to protect their creations, for the weak will always take from the strong, burdening and weakening families, passing frailty and dependency onto the next generation. It is the world's greatest tragedy that so many young must die, but it ensures our descendants do not grow vulnerable.'*
>
> *'Do you think I will be strong?'* Follows asked his father.
>
> *'You've survived so far. Age grows strength, experience cultivates knowledge, failure and success teach fortitude, and although you have seen only twelve winters, you've begun to accumulate all these. But time cannot impart will, and without it your strength and knowledge are ineffectual. You will be shaped by experience, work, suffering, and triumph, and you will become a man, individual in habit and thought. But will decides your life. If others are stronger or*

more cunning, they will dominate you and dispossess you of the life you desire. Men will try and kill you, outmanoeuvre you, and only your will can determine your resistance. Courage determines will, and courage is a choice. How strong an adult you become is your choice.'

As his father had promised, many men had tried to kill him, but he had survived, proving he was not weak. He found his father's face difficult to recall. Time had faded his father's memory, and Quiet had replaced his image. But he still felt his father's company, like a watchfulness still assessing him. Occasionally he found himself acting to impress his father, hoping each achievement proved he possessed the strength his father had reiterated so important. One day he hoped his father's spirit would regard him as an equal and be proud.

His drifted aimlessly through his past, his memories warm company. His reflections gradually became dreamlike, closing his eyes and sagging his limbs. He was on the brink of sleep when a flicker in his periphery alerted him.

An experienced fear awoke immediately, stilling him vigilant, exhaustion gone. Through the long grasses, he stared after the light and saw an occasional glimmer escape the trees. It was a campfire; there were people nearby.

Their proximity was terrifying. The surroundings had given him no indication of predators or people. They must have approached through the forest; a small group capable of moving silently. They had buried their fire in the forest to remain hidden, but the gaps in the trees had conspired against them. A fire's warmth was unnecessary, which meant they were cooking. Cooking this late suggested they had travelled without eating, so were probably running from something and exhausted.

His assessment settled him, the situation controlled. His

presence was unknown and the proceedings of his choosing. But the realisation that women could be close surfaced and reawakened longing's pain. Solitude's frustration overpowered thoughts of escape and fuelled his desperation to investigate the group. He could not miss an opportunity to end the unhappiness of wasting feelings. A violent urge to end his loneliness fanatically grew and committed him to risk himself.

He needed to assess the men and the feasibility of taking their women. The fire would worsen the people's night vision and allow him to stalk their perimeter hidden. So he followed the firelight into the forest, eyes fixed to its glow, his feet examining the ground to avoid sound. The forest canopy starved his surroundings of light and buried him in shadows. He shifted through the underbrush with practised grace, encroaching only when sure of secrecy. Occasionally he stopped to listen, aware that the dark could also hide others, but silence greeted each pause and allowed him to continue.

Soon the murmur of people found him. His excitement grew but he forced calm. He crouched lower until finally crawling, confining his approach to the densest undergrowth where people would not likely visit. Slowly he laboured into a viewpoint where firelight could not reveal him. Cowering in blackness and undergrowth, through breaks in the trees, he saw nine people, but eight faded from notice immediately.

He was captivated and drowned in desire. He forgot his surroundings, blind to anything besides the girl sitting twenty paces away. He felt sick and disarmed and hurt by his many seasons alone. Unmanageable feelings suffocated him: adoration, affection, lust, passion, loneliness, and devotion. He could not leave without her.

She had seen about thirteen winters, her hair light brown and long; her female body weakened him and provoked a sorrow that stole his strength. He was unable to disengage from her, rooted to her softness and the differences they shared. He struggled for sense, knowing his coherence was damaged. He had to retreat to compose.

He backed into the forest, ashamed by his discomposure. When suitably distant, he slumped against a tree, overrun by desperation, eyes shut, breathing pained.

After a time, the quiet helped steady him. He had been unprepared for such feeling and had been made defenceless if discovered. Restoring objectivity was difficult, but he was able to rescue some clarity. He returned to his situation. There had been eight people besides the girl: an older couple, a young couple, two children, a very scarred man, and an old woman. The mood was sullen and each face apprehensive.

The older couple's man had seen about forty winters and his woman about thirty-five. They had looked tired, the man particularly worn. The young couple had both seen around twenty winters, the little girl and boy presumably theirs, seven and four winters respectively. The woman was midpregnancy. The younger man was tall and sinewy, probably the older couple's son since men usually remained with their families and women joined their partner's group.

The scarred man had seen about thirty-five winters and was probably brother to one of the older couple. The firelight had illuminated his damage: his scars, missing eye, and three missing fingers. But despite these injuries, his dangerousness was unquestionable. He was the most heavyset, stained, and familiar with violence. He sat quietly, confident and natural, deliberately peripheral.

The old woman was withdrawn from the conversation and on the precipice of sleep. She looked haggard by a demanding life and not long for the world. She was without a partner, meaning she had survived on family support.

Then there was the girl who had captivated him so completely. She was likely daughter to the older couple and possibly sister to the younger man. She did not have a partner, which was peculiar since she would have attracted considerable male attention.

If the group was only these nine people, she would have paired with the scarred man, yet she sat alone, without children or even pregnant. The group were escaping something, but it was unlikely the girl would have left behind a partner or children. These observations led him to believe the girl was the cause of the family's situation. And given her age, singlehood, and the family's situation, it seemed feasible that a disagreement between a suitor and her family had escalated into conflict and forced their escape. This explained the group's situation and dejection.

He wondered if the girl had realised her prospects were suddenly limited and that her likely partner's age promised a long widowhood and family dependency. If she wished to escape her situation, she might not resist her abduction; he was a younger and less debilitated partner.

She would initially be afraid, but he would endear himself with affection, provisions, and protection. She would learn he was committed, and he would earn her admiration. She would bear their children and lend their lives depth, and he would work to ensure they were never hungry.

He had been unprepared for such feelings and unsuspecting that his ambition could be so quickly diverted. She had reawakened deep wants, intensified his loneliness, and lessened the Settlement's necessity. She had become all important and death an acceptable risk to take her.

He had no choice but to abduct her. Peacefully approaching her family was too dangerous, as people were impulsive and erratic. She might also already have admirers, which would incite violent defence of her. If he followed the family until he could meet her alone, coaxing her away was unlikely—being confronted by a heavily scarred adult male, unequipped with her language, would terrify her. He had to incapacitate and carry her away.

Possessed with a plan, he felt more composed. He crept back to the group and into the same cover. From his hideaway he watched the girl, captivated, her unconscious grace painful.

After a while the family finally settled to sleep, the fire was extinguished, and conversation postponed. She faded into the night, leaving only her shape. Scant moonlight found the clearing through the broken canopy, illuminating only outlines. When someone rose, their shape found contrast with the forest and informed him who had risen. Some family members rose and relieved themselves during the night, leaving him hopeful she might soon have similar need and separate herself.

He waited for any opportunity, vigilant through the night, unencumbered by tiredness, roused by desire and nervousness. If unsuccessful tonight, he would trail the family until an opportunity arose, but he hoped this unnecessary: the longer his pursuit the more likely his detection.

As the night aged, he grew restless, aware first light meant retreat into hiding. He considered a rapid assault to kill the men, but despite their unpreparedness, he doubted he would succeed. Further, killing the girl's family would destroy any chance of gaining her affection. So instead he waited for dawn and retreat.

The darkness began thinning and light began invading. He was readying to steal away when the girl moved. She stood and wandered sleepily from the group. Invigorated, he backed into the trees, soundlessly circling to intercept her. He moved impetuously, sacrificing stealth for speed. Finally, he found her silhouette. As he neared, she sleepily turned towards his rustle, still bleary and inattentive.

He lunged towards her, scaring her rigid, disarmed of defence or reaction. He gripped her throat to stop her scream and struck her unconsciousness. Now that he had her silence, he had to escape before her absence was noticed and the manhunt began. He summoned all his urgency, collected the girl upon his shoulders, and beat towards the grass outside the forest.

With the night waning, and discovery of the girl's absence imminent, he doubted he would escape far before the chase began; but this did not deter him. Frightened at losing her, he threw himself violently forwards.

He landed upon the grassland and sprinted for the nearby rocky mountains. The rock would leave no tracks and would temporarily secret his escape, earning him some time. But the dark blue of morning was already scattering the darkness and revealing his trail through the trees.

He drove up the mountain, his fear overpowering his protesting legs and his weighted ascent saturated in terror. But he would not yield for any small relief until distant. He contoured upwards, racing against the lifting dark, his exertion fanatical.

As the ethereal twilight descended, his feet found the summit, encouraging him to believe that escape was possible.

SIX

THE MOUNTAIN RANGE SOARED above the sea of trees and wound towards the waking sun. He hurtled along its ridgeline, leaving no tracks upon the stone. Fresh winds wrapped around him, their currents kind despite the early morning chill. The dusk faded as sunlight pierced the horizon and coloured the sky. With dawn's arrival, he had to leave the exposed ridge—he was too visible. But he postponed, needing his height to search for streams to hide his route.

He ran onward, scouring the lightening land. His body strained under the load, his chest heaved for air, and his overloaded legs buckled. Sweat soaked him, but he bore the pain and allowed no respite.

That was when she stirred. He tore behind a protruding rock, guarding them from anyone looking upon the mountain. He propped the girl against the rock, and waited nervously, unsure how to manage her waking. Her head bobbed unsteadily, and her eyes struggled themselves open. She deliriously examined her surroundings as her mind slowly surfaced, briefly meeting his eyes, unregistering, still not fully returned.

Her beauty again disarmed him and made the world disappear. She was painful to behold, her femininity both fascinating and wounding. He felt an ugly contrast: scarred, weathered, and hard. He thought himself undeserving, his male qualities inferior, making him want to overcome his unworthiness and win her with care and tenderness.

Against her graceful features, her swollen temple chastised him, but force had been necessary so he suppressed guilt—it would encumber their escape. Despite his urgency, he waited for her lucidity; he could not escape by indefinitely incapacitating and carrying her. He needed her acquiescence, by force or intimidation if necessary, otherwise he would be caught and killed. He would not retreat to suffer loneliness and live knowing his cowardice was the cause.

Unthinkingly, he reached out and stroked her cheek: her softness so different from his taut skin. The peculiarity of their being two types of humans assailed him. Each sex was built and behaved so differently, yet they desired and enriched each other. Their fortunes were intertwined despite their differences, bound together through hardship and elation, united by support and dependence. Their symbiosis was another unfathomable contrivance of the gods, a device that deepened man's existence.

He waited anxiously, unsure how to convey his affection when she woke in terror. He retrieved meat from his pack and held it ready to present to her. His other hand brushed her hair, hoping this would communicate his fondness.

Slowly, her eyes reacquired understanding, her head righted, and their gazes met. A moment of confusion flickered across her face before fear enveloped her. Her eyes widened, tears brimmed, her breath drew in sharply, and her hands covered her face.

As she cowered into herself, his caress fell away, his impotence to lessen her fear difficult to bear. Her sobs were weakening, drowning his dreams of shared affection, family, and companionship. He believed he could provide her the contentment her family could not, but without her compliance their beginning was impossible.

She clasped her legs to her chest and bowed her head to hide her face. He watched her dejectedly but could not leave; the world was empty without her. He would force her onwards. She might despise and fear him, but one day she would understand and forgive him, and then their lives together could begin. He would bear her hate and make amends in time.

He stowed away the meat and carefully raised her to standing, struggling to avoid compounding her distress. She neither resisted nor attempted escape, disabled to inaction by fear. She kept her face hidden and her sobs suffocated in hands. Gently, he lowered her hands and raised her head, bringing her eyes to meet his.

They silently searched each other, the predicament surreal, each cautious. Her regard was unclear, but he saw some self-possession—afraid but collected. He spoke, aware she would not speak his language, hoping instead his voice would communicate his feeling. Evoking all his warmth he whispered, 'Don't be afraid. Come with me. I cannot live fully without you.'

Their eyes held inside the quiet. He watched her examining him, uneasy but not overcome. Despite their different languages, he felt he had conveyed his feelings. She was an adult and aware of adult practices; their age, sex, and situation made obvious his intentions, which he hoped would also defend his actions. If she accepted his behaviour had been necessary, forgiveness would quickly follow. If she also appreciated her prospects with her family were poor, she would realise him a fortunate opportunity, and then his kindness and provision would win her affection.

The passing time was endangering him, and he needed her to quickly join his escape. He took her hand, she nervously watching, her distress reduced to streaks of drying tears. Whether motivated by fear or curiosity, when he stepped forward, she joined him, and together they strode along the ridge towards the sunrise, his thumb gratefully brushing her hand.

He coaxed them into a run atop the world. Sun swept over them, revealing enormous forests and grasslands. Water twisted through the vast plains into the horizons, while hills and valleys churned the ground. The sky was clear, the morning blue, and the sun's touch relaxing despite the situation. Under growing heat, they ascended and descended the peaks alongside one another, occasionally inspecting each other.

Accustomed to sleep deprivation, it troubled him little. Immersed in flight, his hunger disappeared; he would not eat or rest until distant and hidden. He concentrated instead on looking for rivers near their mountain, and after a time he saw one. His eyes followed it across the lowland until it disappeared into a forest; it was the opportunity he needed.

He slowed them to a standstill and invited the girl closer. Amenably she neared, though cautious and presumably still scared. He saw her fear—captive to his will and coerced into escape—but he was unworried; time would heal. He pointed towards the river, and she inspected his route and understood.

Her composure, despite her situation, increased his veneration. But when she noticed his admiration she shied away, head bowed and expression inexpressive. Trying to inspire trust and calm, he brushed the damp hair from her face, affectionately smoothing it behind her ears. When she seemed more relaxed, he gently took her hand and guided her down the mountain.

They contoured downward onto the lowland and followed the river's whirring sound through sun-warmed grasses. They carved a trail, but he chanced that it would go unnoticed by any pursers on the ridge. If wrong, his route and escape strategy would be revealed, and being caught likely.

They continued until the grass tapered away into mossy riverbanks, and they plunged into the pebble-bedded waters, submerging to their knees, their steps quickened by the currents. Heavy foliage lined the banks, disguising them from view, lessening his anxiety. The river swept them through plain and valley, guiding them towards the forest downriver. They marched, speckled by sun and shade, the forest's detail quickly emerging. He looked back upon the mountain for pursuers, but the sunlit mountain stood alone and still.

They pushed the mountain behind, steps lumbering and heavy, the walk tiring but slowly bringing the forest closer. They waded onward until underneath stretching boughs and overhanging trees, between the labyrinth of oaks, beeches, and birches. Sunshine fell between the canopy gaps onto leafed floors; collapsed trees interwove their standing companions. The forest's tranquillity encouraged their quiet, leaving the currents to sing unchallenged and fill the forest.

He kept them in the river, deciding it too soon to create tracks. They navigated each fall and rapid, urgency depressed by the forest's peace, beating onward until their river dispersed into a lake. They stopped alongside, gazing over the tree-encircled surface. Overhead, the sun reached its highest, the day half over. He looked at the girl and saw her tiredness. She looked up at him, examining him, wary. He wanted to embrace and reassure her, but feared such invasiveness would alarm her; so instead he kept distance, hoping his restraint would earn her trust.

He led them onto the soil shoreline and followed its perimeter, moving amongst the stillness and sunbeams, watching leaves ripple the lake and bubbles burst the surface. He looked for streams leaving the lake, planning to follow and fish them before dark. They skirted the shore until he found them. They followed the streams and bush-covered banks, along the earth beach, negotiating the underbrush and jutting trees, until stony falls interrupted them. Their stream cascaded into a lagoon beneath, its shallows promising good fishing. They climbed down stone cliffs to the pool, the sun now half descended.

He invited the girl to rest while he fished, and so she shuffled into comfort against a fallen tree. He retrieved his last meat for her, and she timidly ate, eyes averted. He knew she still feared for her safety, but without words he had only gestures to communicate goodwill. She did seem less worried now; perhaps she was beginning to recognise him as safe.

Leaving the girl to eat, he stepped into the water, dipping to his knees, spear poised to strike. Time passed easily—the forest cool, the water calm, and the wait pleasant. The first fish that swam past him met his spearhead and found itself upon the bank. Then he reassumed readiness, spear held overhead.

He was aware of the girl watching him, assessing him and her safety. He avoided her gaze, not wanting to interrupt her inspection. This was her opportunity to consider him as a partner and recognise the prospects he offered. If she could approve of him, intimacy and investment would follow.

He trawled the water until the world began dimming. Four fish lay upon the bank. He left the water to cook before darkness made a fire imprudent. He built a fireplace and coaxed the dead wood into flame, wrapping them both in warmth. He skewered the fish above the fire, and they waited impatiently. When cooked, he passed the girl the first fish. She ate greedily, her enthusiasm encouraging—she was relaxing in his company. They ate quickly, subduing hunger's pleadings.

Once finished, he scattered the fireplace to disguise their stay, then turned to the girl and found her waiting. Pause made apparent how perfect she was. Her beauty was difficult to bear, and he wondered if she realised how she weakened him. He smiled at her, vulnerable to her reaction. She watched him, unmoving and unreadable. He approached and stroked her hair, watching her breathing quicken. But she held his gaze, intimidated by his potential danger but recognising his fondness.

He interrupted himself, knowing the time to cover distance was disappearing. He took them deeper into the trees, following the brook into thickening dark. As they walked, the light began thinning until they were wandering in blackness. When they happened upon a clearing, he stopped them, deciding it time to sleep. They adjusted into comfort upon the leaf floor, streaked by moonlight, the stream's rustle alongside. He offered the girl furs, which she wrapped herself within and lay upon.

Moonlight slipped the broken canopy and tinted their outlines. They lay facing, faces shadowed. His eyes skirted her torso, prisoner to her shape. Without distractions, his desire welled and overwhelmed. His mind slowly drowned in lust. Urges reached from suppressed depths and suffocated all other thoughts, restraint awful and saddening. The lonely seasons hurt, and he remembered all his wasted wants.

His hand reached out and fell upon her chest. He felt her breathing quicken, but she remained still. The dark hid her expression and reaction, momentarily slowing his advance. He moved closer and embraced her. Her breaths wisped across his chest and her warmth trembled in his arms. He caressed her and felt her nervousness and knew she understood his intentions.

He removed their clothes and held her, their nakedness touching: warm, soft, and elating. He kissed her, and she did not resist. He knew not whether her compliance was born from survival or attraction, but he proceeded impulsively, exploring her under mixed shadow and moonlight. He took her on the forest floor, overtaken by passion and ache.

The half-Moon wandered across the night sky, her light barely finding them, leaving them only touch to explore each other. At the culmination of their encounter, he held her, protective and possessive, overcome by an unfamiliar contentment. She fell asleep in his arms, and shortly he joined her. He drifted into dreams until morning woke them together in the same embrace.

SEVEN

FIRST LIGHT FELL BETWEEN the branches onto his nakedness and nudged him from sleep. He opened his eyes to breeze-shuffled leaves and sunbeam shards. Their entwined bodies lay underneath furs and sunrise, his waking almost dreamlike. Feeling the girl in his arms flooded him with relief; she and their intimacy had not been imagined.

But morning's clarity brought reality. His escape had lost urgency—his rests had been too long and his pace too leisurely. If his pursuers had been relentless and diligent, they would be close, and their numbers made his survival unlikely. His desire and her beauty had damaged his judgement and endangered him, but being with her had helped moderate his enchantment and revived his pragmatism. But he would never abandon her to save himself. She had lessened the Settlement's importance, yet fulfilled him. He just needed to reinvigorate their escape, or his fulfilment would be brief.

His stirring woke her, and she turned to glimpse him through heavy eyelids. She wore drowsy scrutiny, communicating neither fear nor affection, but her reserve had lessened, cheering him. His arousal quickly resurfaced, but he resisted—escape was the priority. He gently disentangled from the girl and rose. She raised herself also, bristling against morning's cold, and began readying to leave. As they dressed and gathered their possessions, he disguised their stay by smoothing the body-depressed earth. When finished, he embraced the girl, wanting to assure her of his commitment and fondness. She did not embrace him, but he felt her easiness. He smiled, retrieved his spears, and invited her to follow him into the forest.

The morning was cool; the only sounds were twigs cracking, leaves rustling, and the stream. Slowly, the sun grew higher, and richer colours invaded, brightening their path. He pushed them fast, compensating for yesterday, only stopping to eat grubs and plants and to quench thirsts. But as the sun summitted, he realised their pace was unsustainable without substantial food. He had felt his own disagreeableness growing, and knew hers would follow, potentially supplanting her amenableness with reluctance; he needed to hunt and rest her.

Through the day he scoured their trail for signs of animals, but he saw nothing. As the sun lowered, his frustration grew, and he became nervous of the girl's mood; but finally, the forest provided. A deer's whine echoed from downstream, alleviating his anxiety.

He stopped them, needing stealth to proceed. He looked at the girl—her attentions had livened and little frustration remained. She had heard, and been invigorated, by the deer. Their eyes met with understanding, his enthusiasm to hunt encouraged by her eagerness.

He motioned she wait while he hunted, and though he realised their separation gave her an opportunity to escape, he doubted she would. Once alone, she would weigh her future with him, against her future without him, and would realise he could give her fulfilment and purpose. Though fear might influence her, he was an opportunity for an adult relationship. She was possibly already pregnant and he the father, and he was a willing provider; she might never encounter such again.

The girl nodded and sat beside the stream, amongst the moss and leaves. He gave her his pack, took up his spears, gestured farewell, and began towards the deer. He moved delicately and gradually disappeared from the girl. He crept downstream, shifting between the trees, until he heard more deer ahead. His eyes rummaged for the quietest route and his steps followed. Then he saw a deer's hind legs through the nest of trunks. He lifted his spear ready, his breathing quickened, and his aggression rose.

He slid from cover and hurled his spear at the nearest deer. Before the herd noticed him, his spear tore into a doe, shocking it frozen. The doe's legs buckled, and he raised his second spear to finish her, but panic struck the herd and began their stampede. He threw his spear, but the rushing herd deflected it into the shore, giving the doe opportunity to compose and retreat. The doe joined the stampede and stumbled through the stream into the trees.

Annoyed, but accepting the chase, he sprinted in pursuit. He burst through the stream, snatched up his spear, and hurtled into the forest. The doe would slow and collapse eventually, it would not escape. He darted amongst the trees, guided by tracks and blood. Occasionally, he saw the doe, lurching and heaving, then pushing onwards. He pursued her relentlessly, focused and closing on the kill.

Finally, he found the doe fallen and struggling to stand. He flung his spear into the deer and punctured her back. The deer reeled wildly, eyes fear-emblazoned, whines alarmed and choked. She crashed into the ground, spasms vicious and contorted. But the injury quickly slowed the deer to stillness. Finally, she lay unmoving, dark eyes wandering, chest slowly rising and falling.

He approached alongside, quiet and respectful of her last moments. He stroked her, wanting to spare her further suffering, watching her docile eyes drift. The kill always lowered his aggression, always sombre and cause for sympathy and reflection. Subdued, he waited away the doe's life. He wondered about the girl and was nervous about their separation, but he reassured himself that she would wait if rational. He suppressed worry; he could not affect the outcome now. He listened as the herd's galloping grew distant and disappeared, leaving only a nearby stream's trickle. As the doe died, he looked towards the water and was immediately alarmed.

The scarred man sprinted past, about sixty paces away, presumably hunting to sustain the chase, oblivious to Follows. Knowing the conflict he had hoped to avoid was inevitable, violence consumed Follows. He had been tracked too close to escape, but the gods had given him an opportunity to strike first, and fear would not dissuade him.

As the scarred man disappeared, Follows ripped a spear from the deer and chased after him, running parallel with him, hidden behind trees. He doubted the scarred man had slept, but this gave him no advantage: exertion would moderate his tiredness and prime his opponent. But fortunately, the scarred man was also unsuspecting and distracted.

Follows raced forward, hurtling over obstacles, gaining until the scarred man emerged into view. Follows strafed through the trees until behind the scarred man. The scarred man glanced backwards, startled by the footsteps, too late to save himself from the spear careering towards him. Follows' weapon ruptured the scarred man's back and threw him to the ground, frightened and bewildered. Before the scarred man could compose himself, fists exploded into his face. His world darkened, never to return.

Follows rose gasping, relieved and elated by victory, his tension easing. He went to retrieve his spear when something collided into his thigh. His leg was heaved from underneath him, and he fell, stunned and confused. He looked at his leg—gouged and dripping blood onto the leaves and earth. He looked around for explanation and saw the bloodied spear that had injured him; further attacks were coming.

Then he was set upon. Punches struck his head onto stones, damaging his clarity and ability to fight. His arms instinctively wrapped around his head, but the fists crashed through. Panic ripped through Follows. He reflexively reached out and embraced his enemy, pinning the attacking arms. Despite his clouded mind, Follows realised death was close—awaking a maniacal survivalism.

His opponent wrested free and ripped at Follows' eyes and face, but Follows instinctively lashed out. Follows again grasped the man to his chest and sunk his teeth into his throat. He ground through flesh and sinew and into bone, drenching them both in blood. A livid madness erupted from Follows, and a frenzied scream escaped his gnashing teeth. He tore out the man's throat and spat out the bone and flesh. The man contorted in agony, writhing helplessly. Follows dived upon him, unable to recognise the fight over, deranged by trauma; death had never been so close.

His hands crushed bone and tore flesh, spraying blood, cutting his knuckles, until finally his ferocity exhausted. Follows was disturbed and shaking, hunched over his lifeless opponent. Overwhelmed, he screamed skyward, tears streaking his blood-smeared face. He broke and crumpled between the two dead men, his eyes closed, his trembling hands holding his head. He cried until empty, horrified by his life's fragility.

Behind shaking fingers his cries ebbed into sobs and his breathing slowed. His hands fell from his face, dragging bloody trails across his cheeks. He lay upon the earth and stone, staring vacantly at the canopy dancing oblivious to the bloodshed beneath. The stream sang beside him, echoing through the forest. The Wind God caressed him, whispering to him, asking him to remember his strength.

He lay watching sunbeams slip between the leaves and stretch to the ground, shifting as the branches swayed. Slowly the calm restored his control, his stupor waned, and sanity returned. He was hurt but alive, time would heal him, his wounds would fade. Today would become memory, and his life with the girl would continue.

The girl was too distant and the forest too dense for his screams to find her. He imagined her resting beside the brook, full of sleep and hunger, waiting unawares. He would blame his wounds on a protective stag and return the doe's meat as evidence of the fight and victory. He could live with the girl without fearing her family, ease their pace, and build their relationship. But if absconded, she was lost—encumbered by injury he would not catch her.

He looked at the culprit of his trauma, dead and butchered, his drained eyes staring into the void. It was the worn old man—the girl's likely father. The young man's threat remained, but he doubted he had also pursued. The young man had probably stayed to protect his family; the women and children were dead if all the men were lost. Their family would endure, survival was ingrained and obstinate.

He stood, desperate to leave the battleground, his eyes avoiding the dead. He followed the shore until the dead men were hidden downstream, stumbling each alternate step, blood-soaked and sweating, frayed flesh dripping, skin cold. He focused on the routine to mend himself, confining the fight to memory. His limbs were weak, close to collapse, his weight shifting mostly onto his uninjured leg.

He began gathering for a fire, each movement painful and stiff. He needed to seal his wound, clean himself, and hide his injury's severity. He wanted the girl confident of his strength, otherwise she would feel vulnerable and insecure; such would damage her affection for him. She could never know her family had been killed; she would hate him, and any chance of gaining her trust would be destroyed. Separation might follow, benefitting neither of them. She might also never accept the deaths were unintentional, tainting their future with suspicion. He wanted only her, and he would not revisit loneliness and introversion to be unconstructively honest.

He quickly sourced the components for a fire and built his hearth. He coaxed flame onto wood and placed a spearhead beside it. He waited, staring into the fire, thoughts avoiding the coming pain. He picked up the spearhead and nestled it into his wound. His flesh screamed and his stomach churned; a cold sweat emerged, and he vomited. He persevered until the bleeding stopped.

When finished, he washed in the stream. His legs were unsteady, his body clammy and senses disorientated. He rinsed his furs of blood and cleaned his wound. He steadied his thoughts and gradually composed. He donned the sodden furs, their damp pleasant upon his flustered skin. Feeling weak but better, he returned to the doe. He knelt to carve her, finding strength difficult to muster. He pulled his spear from her and cut away enough meat to last him and the girl several days. He shouldered the meat and began towards the girl, struggling under his load, pushing through the difficulty, driven onwards by the memory of her beauty.

The journey riled and debilitated him further, but he continued until he arrived at the stream where he had encountered the herd. He waded into the cold water, spirited on by rest, food, and her. He laboured upstream through the trees, fighting the increasing strain. Dread was building. If she was gone, he had nothing. He would have been tempted with happiness then deprived. He hid from the thought, too drained to bear it.

Then, as he grew closer, a break in the trees revealed the girl asleep under furs. The world faded and left only her. He forgot his pain, and his dreams of family and affection felt within reach. His mood rallied and his last steps felt easy. He arrived by her side, close to collapse, but uplifted. He laid the meat quietly down, not wanting to disturb her. He silently crafted a fireplace then reluctantly struck stones together, pouring sparks onto tinder.

The crack woke the girl, and her eyes opened. She inspected his cuts and bruises, disquieted by his wounds. She stayed still, watching him from beneath furs. Cheered by her company, he animatedly acted through a fight with a stag, concluding the explanation of his wounds with his triumph.

The girl barely reacted and remained uneasy. He saw she understood his story but was too wary to respond. Her reserve made a trusting relationship seem faraway, causing his enthusiasm to fade, and his exhaustion to reassert. Too tired to rally much spirit, he sat and tended to the fire. The girl saw his dejection but offered nothing. They sat quietly, attentions swimming the flames, both feeling the sullen atmosphere. When the fire was ready, he skewered the meat and cooked, his day's last ambition to feed them.

Overhead, the dying day relinquished its pale blue for red-streaked dusk. Crimson light spilled through the trees and ignited their stream, colouring the forest floor in blushing dark and reddening their skin. The evening wind dipped through the trees, shivering the couple, encouraging them under furs.

Finally, they gorged, famished by the day, moods drained. The food restored some strength, but sleep was overtaking them. The fire made heavy their eyes and limbs, and sleep seduced them. They looked at each other, both wearing tiredness. She was all he wanted, and knowing her trust and fondness were still distant saddened him. He needed her friendship and intimacy, and feared an existence without them. He could only treat her kindly and hope that her fear would fade and her affection build. Their eyes agreed to sleep, and under scorched heavens, they reclined upon the earth, separate until his hand found hers. They held until sleep, collapsed before the red sky had faded to black.

They slept until dawn roused them, and they reluctantly left their furs. Every movement stabbed him with pain, and every effort was strained. He grimaced against the discomfort, packed his possessions, and readied. Then the couple left under sunrise.

He limped, incapable of speed. But despite the pain, he felt unburdened. He was free from pursers, his every step accompanied by her, his loneliness left in the past. He was weak and enfeebled, but strength would return. He carried the scars and cost of victory, each jolt of pain a promise of a better life to come.

EIGHT

THE SUBSEQUENT DAYS DRIFTED by easily, each temperate and restful. The stream closely followed the Settlement's path, doubling as a guide through the forest. The kind days cradled the couple through awkward beginnings, making survival easy and the time together relaxed.

While they walked amongst the trees and underbrush, he began teaching her his language, striving to build friendship. The girl listened and endeavoured to learn, but remained guarded, hiding behind reserve. With each indicated object, feature, and action, he named it and she repeated it, attempting to remember its sound. He tutored without tiring, encouraged by the merest progress, excited by the prospect of conversing with her. She began asking the names of objects, phenomena, and expressions; and he would construct sentences to demonstrate his language's structure. Gradually, she braved his language to express herself.

His injuries often forced their rest, but she was patient with his weakness, showing no restlessness or annoyance. It was a charity that simultaneously embarrassed him and endeared her to him. Ashamed of his limitation, he disguised his discomfort, labouring to project a strength he did not possess, wanting her to feel safer in his company. Despite his incapacity, he pushed himself, wanting to use the days productively. Gradually rest and time healed him, and his legs became strong again.

Finding him kind, the girl's defensiveness slowly grew less. As her reticence wore away, her naturalness surfaced, allowing familiarity and her attraction to build. They became adept at reading each other, learnt each other's character, manner, and idiosyncrasies. Their personalities pliably accommodated one another; the other's thoughts and feelings grew recognisable, and a considerate dynamic emerged.

Every habit of hers succeeded only to increase his fondness: swaying to her own whistling, hiding her face when laughing, studying her food before eating, holding her breath when surprised. One morning, he watched her sit under the sun, eyes closed, thoughts elsewhere, and he felt blessed.

Youthful attraction and curiosity hastened their union, bridging the gulf of language and conquering restraint. The rains also brought them closer, interrupting their travel to encourage them under cover without task. They would huddle by a fire, serenaded by rainfall, spirits calmed, thoughts quieted, bodies close, and curious eyes meeting. They would stir each other's desires and succumb to them. His caress usually breached their divide, running fingers through her hair, hands tracing her body, arms pulling her close. Curious touch would ignite into exploration and press them lustfully together. In the aftermath of their encounters, she lay in his arms, both quiet and gratified.

When not consorting, sheltering, or resting, they ambled through the lazy days side by side, growing more comfortable and natural with each setting sun. The days and nights rose and fell weightlessly without incident, blending into a dreamlike stream unmarried to time or order.

They navigated forest, plain, and mountain, feeling the summer cool, watching the leaves yellow, redden, and brown. They enjoyed the disappearing summer's easy provision. They fished, he hunted—neither hungry long. The night skies were clear, allowing them to settle unsheltered, watching the stars together. They progressed without drive, enjoying the present, subdued by the intoxication of initial partnership. Existence felt unreal and ordinary life transcended. He indulged unreservedly, fearing this fulfilment temporary.

Time passed and the Sun God grew weaker. The leaves began wilting and falling, colouring the ground, stripping the trees. The wind blew cooler and the nights were less kind. The summer was dying and the time to prepare for the Winter God's reign was nearing.

Their last days of travel took them through an enormous forest, the hunting still easy but the cold growing more bitter. On their last day of travelling, they woke on the forest's edge near huge grasslands. Under dawn light, they stared at the silhouetted mountains across these plains, knowing they would yield them caves. He would use the peaks to choose them a refuge near forests and lakes, so winter scavenging would be easier. There was sufficient time before the snows to make a cave comfortable. It was time to camp; he would not risk their safety and comfort to cover more distance.

He examined the morning sky, benign and vast; the day would be dry and visibility good for crossing the grassland. Man was weak prey, but vigilance was some protection. The ground was flat, making ambushes hard for predators and giving him time for strategy. There was no reason not to proceed.

He turned to the girl and found her smiling, ready to begin for the mountains. With gazes held, they left. The leaf littered ground and starved trees fell behind as dew-soaked grasses nuzzled each step. In the distance, hundreds of bison grazed, overhead birds sang. They looked for signs of predators, but saw none, allowing them to continue relaxed.

They walked without pause, eager to explore the mountains,

discussing how to prepare their home, their imaginations building havens from blizzards. He would fill their cave with furs and tools, and then enjoy the remaining summer. They could watch the days shorten and nights lengthen, exchanging histories, painting their home with stories of gods and themselves. When the snows enveloped, they could hide under furs, appreciating each other while her pregnancy progressed, enjoying their fires, and sleeping late. In previous winters, the same surroundings, thoughts, and routine had attacked his sanity; but this winter he was unafraid of these.

They walked, enjoying the sunlight, the mountains growing larger and the forest distant. They ate dried meats, watched for threats, and talked quietly until finally they arrived at the mountain's foothills. The sun was falling, but enough time remained to search the mountain. They waded up the rock, the slope gradual and barren. They summited the world together, paused and stirred by its enormity.

The chain of mountains straggled forests and plains, the crests an irregular procession connected by shallow depressions. They saw an immense lake drinking the surrounding streams, bordered by horizon reaching prairies. Near the lake spread a huge forest that promised both prey and provisions. A shelter near the forest, the lake, and the grassland would serve them best. Discussion was unnecessary, they both knew a winter shelter's requirements.

They embarked down the mountain, searching for any fissure or cavern that could accommodate them. The sinking sun tinged their hair and skin in auburn light, and burned the lake in crimson colour, seemingly aflame. Upon the plains, a family of mammoth walked towards the forest, black against the flushed grasses, shadows stretched thin. The couple watched the confident giants amble across the reddening ground, mesmerised by the size of the world's masters, coveting their freedom from danger, grateful of their tolerance until challenged.

Under bloody sun, they traversed flowing foothills, interweaving the slope climbing trees. They searched until they found a slender crack a small climb above the ground. Its dark scar was obvious against the flat rockface. Its climb and length were a man's height, its width was half a man; easy to defend, and to barricade against cold. Tall evergreens patrolled around the entrance, vowing to conceal their fires and shield them from winds.

He climbed into the opening, arms outstretched, eyes adjusting to the dark. The cave unevenly deepened, fifteen paces long and ten paces wide, the ground mostly flat, the curved walls smooth. Long cracks were scored into the ceiling, possibly extending to the outside, ideal for evacuating campfire smoke. The cave was a good discovery; they could be comfortable here.

He stood at the entrance and met the girl's questioning look. Not wanting to influence her opinion, he invited her inspection, and she eagerly climbed and disappeared inside. When finished, she appeared in the sunlit entrance, bathed in red sunlight, wearing an approving smile.

They sat against the cave walls under the sanguine sun, committed to sedentariness for the remaining day. They ate dried meat and fruits beside each other, thoughts drifting until he spoke.

'What should we call our home?' he asked.

She searched for something appropriate, until she smiled decidedly.

'The Burning Red,' she said assuredly.

He approved. Immersed in failing red light, their cave and mountain dyed in warmth, the name faultlessly captured their shelter. Subsequent use would evoke memories of their arrival and the setting.

After eating, they huddled together under furs and watched the darkness drown the day until they fell into each other's affections. Afterwards they lay awake, hugged together, alone with their thoughts, tired eyes cast into the star filled skies, peacefully awaiting sleep.

The dark world was still, tinted in white moonlight, sedate and clear. The Moon travelled the Night God's skies, shining and proud. He watched her admiringly, mother to existence, ageless and eternal.

He believed the gods had given him this better life, sympathetic to all his suffering, making amends for his trials and losses. Grateful and reverent, he kept audience as the girl fell asleep. He joined her shortly, subsiding into dreams, content and hopeful.

NINE

SUNRISE PEERED INTO THE cave and onto the sleeping couple, stirring them. Gradually they defeated their drowsiness, rose, and entered the early world. The horizon splintered dawn's light onto their mountain, narrowing their unready eyes.

He inhaled the morning air, enjoying its fresh cold. The girl stood alongside him, stretching away her stiffness, squinting under sunbeams, lifting her mind from sleep. Her light hair trailed her back, braided and shining. The sight of her always mellowed his aggression and made him feel vulnerable and possessive.

He realised his infatuation, but was unable to rationalise it. He would provide and safeguard her without hesitation, not for equivalent care, but to endear himself. Men killed for women, hunted for them, laboured for their comfort and security, so contrarily to men's competitive and violent rivalry towards each other. Men and women were born to different lives, physically incapable of exchanging, helpless without the other to foster a family. They would never understand each other, their experiences and perspectives too dissimilar, but if considerate and affectionate, they were of unequalled comfort to one another.

Under sunrise they parted, venturing to their charges, an

exchanged smile their farewell. He beat towards the lake to fish, hoping to finish quickly so he could explore the area. He turned to watch her disappear into the forest, stepping onto the leaves beneath the brown trees. She faded into shadow, leaving him alone and irrationally forlorn.

He resumed. The air was cold and the forests thin; winter and its imprisonment were near. Usually, he feared winter's sedentariness and introversion. It provoked too much time to think, taunting him with his own mind and past: unrealised ambitions, failures, and losses. He would try to escape in dreams, but was fetched by reality, shown his impermanence and inconsequentiality, reminded of his horrors, and haunted by his brother. Winter was protracted and merciless, sleep a brief respite. After the snows, he emerged, wondering whether he had been strengthened or scarred by enduring himself. But this winter, accompanied by the girl and their growing child, he was no prisoner of himself.

Uplifted by these thoughts, he fell into a run, relishing the softness underfoot and the enfolding cold. His god brushed his skin, encouraging his efforts and elevating his pace. He bounded upon the lake, enjoying his speed and surroundings. The sun cascaded over the freshwater, shimmering each ripple and igniting each stream. He arrived relaxed and warm, and fished the creeks thoughtlessly and automatically. When he had a day's food he departed, impatient to see the girl.

He walked through dead grasses bent by frost, their mountain looming larger. The Burning Red emerged from behind evergreens, already a welcoming sight. As he neared, he saw the girl propped against the rock, scouring a bear fur. She noticed him and smiled. He arrived and laid his fish beside the roots she had gathered. He settled beside her and helped scrub the hide. It was untouched by rot, evidently recently dead: an auspicious find. He postponed exploration; her company was difficult to leave.

They talked playfully while they worked, and teased each other as it latened, without urgency or concern. When dark thickened, they cooked and ate, withdrew early, and slept late. This dynamic became their routine—drive and worry abandoned to enjoy each other.

The days trickled by and blended inextricably into memory. The cave filled with furs for clothing and comfort. They constructed tools for hunting, sewing, carving, painting, and eating. They stockpiled wood for fires, and dried food for any coming scarcities. They ate plentifully while able, preparing their bodies for when food would be scarce.

As winter arrived, the nights lengthened, and the colds attacked more cruelly, compelling them inside earlier. Around fires, they talked and invented games until sleep. They painted their walls with histories of gods, animals, themselves, and the world. When the first snowfall came, their child began kicking. Entranced, he felt its early stirrings, awed by the surreal way humans began. Over the winter, her pregnancy strained her ability to forage and labour, but he compensated, trying to lessen her obligations.

As the snows deepened, they buried meat in ice, building reserves to survive the ungenerous season. When the blizzards came, they barricaded their cave's entrance, plunged beneath furs, cradled each other for warmth, and built fires to defeat the cold.

When storms outlasted their food, he was forced outside to hunt. Huddled beneath furs, he scavenged from the miserly season, setting traps, fishing through broken ice, hunting waylaid by mist and frost, but usually salvaging something.

Slowly the Winter God's excesses grew less, permitting them greater passage into the world. The exertion would better his temperament, making him more patient and affectionate, better humoured, his stories more frequent and optimistic.

When trapped inside, they talked and debated away their

sentence, learning from each other. He explained how humans only aged in winter, how it brought stiffness and sickness, how it slowed and tired people. Summer restored energy, healthy skin, and hair, stirred better moods and sleep. She accepted his explanation, observing that people rarely died in summer, and injuries pained more during winter.

She taught him the origin of the Winter God's cruelty. He was born with an unwanted power that brought cold into existence. His powers brought only death and destruction, earning him ostracism and hatred from the other gods. Hurt by his family's treatment, and wanting only acceptance, he attacked their creations, inflicting his upset and sadness.

They examined eating, never before questioning its necessity. They concluded that within meat was movement, and when consumed, they absorbed and stored this movement. As they moved these reserves emptied, provoking hunger. They realised that sedentary foods, such as plants, fuelled sedentary abilities, such as thoughts and dreams. They saw no way of escaping eating and hunger, and resigned themselves to forever suffer it.

They renamed each other, both believing the other's name an unrepresentative childhood relic. Her family had called her Sleeps Often, but in adulthood it epitomised her little. He named her Mane because of her hair, thick and voluminous like a lion. She instantly approved.

Mane felt Follows unsuitable, regarding him as independent and resilient, like the lone wolves cast out in youth, fashioned strong and autonomous by struggle. Thusly, she named him Wolf.

They recalled their pasts to each other. Her family had been fleeing conflict the night he took her. A high-ranking couple from her previous group had been unable to conceive, causing them to separate. The man sought partnership with Mane, but her father objected to pairing her with a man of suspect fertility. Her father's position offended, and tensions escalated into conflict. Her scarred uncle killed the man, necessitating her family's flight. Two days after the incident was when Follows found her family—and took her.

Follows never told Mane he had killed her uncle and father; her devastation and hate would end their contentment and affection. He empathised with her but could not regret his conduct. He had rescued himself from wasted feelings, begun a family, enriched her life, and was important to someone for the first time since his brother's death.

Mane understood her abduction and forgave him, aware he had chosen the least dangerous way to partner her. Her separation from her family was difficult, but she was objective and judged her situation improved. Despite difficult beginnings, her affection for him was sincere, and she was pleased to be partnered and pregnant. She had also inherited his desire for the Settlement and was excited by its prospect. Infected by his ambition and enthusiasm, her present and future felt richer.

She saw his discomfort when mentioning her family but assured him of her happiness.

'Loss teaches value, Wolf,' she said. 'I used to dread the future, knowing it limited, but now I am unafraid. I will accept whatever the future gives.'

Her confession was moving, her loss relatable, and her perspective humbling. Loss had crippled him, and her outlook filled him with admiration.

'I miss my family, but not my future with them,' Mane continued. 'I wish them easy lives, but I doubt I'll see them again, and that is fine.'

He wanted to comfort her, knowing the cruelty of loss. He did not tell her missing them would grow easier, this was untrue. He told her wounds heal but scars remain, that hurt sporadically revisits, sometimes potently. Loss was a weight forever hauled, a ghost that whispers when it is quiet. Her happiness would endure, but so would her sorrow.

He helped her through difficult reflections by relating his own losses. He told her how he had lost his family, trying to prove that spirit endures.

'I had seen thirteen winters when I lost my parents. It was late winter, the world was thawing, the snow thinning, the sky was clear, and the sun was weak; after a long dark season, even this was uplifting. I had been hunting with my brother, father, and uncle. The men had downed a young bison, and we carried its meat to camp. The day's success left us tired, cheerful, and distracted. We never saw the men waiting behind bushes.

'Two spears collided into both my father and uncle, shocking us all still. My father and uncle fought collapse, standing, blood darkening their furs. My brother and I stood motionless, unsure how to react. Four men emerged from hiding and converged on us, ignoring me and my brother, prioritising the men, knives raised to kill. My father and uncle tried to ignore their injuries, desperate for revenge before death. Blood pooled at their feet, their footprints crimson stains, their faces wearing violence.

'The fight lasted moments. My father managed to spear a man through his stomach and cripple him to the floor. My uncle's body faltered, his spear fell, so he raised his knife. My brother and I attacked with spears, but only my brother's connected, slashing open a man's leg, impeding the man long enough for us to sprint past him. My father and uncle were too weakened to defend themselves; they were slaughtered while we escaped.

'We fled down a hill and disappeared from view a moment before my brother tackled me into an icy river behind some rocks. His tortured eyes found mine and pleaded my silence. The water was agony, numbing everything, stealing breath, and clouding thought. I closed my eyes and imagined myself elsewhere, around campfires listening to stories, eating venison under stars, anything to escape the pain. Behind shut eyes, I heard men run past, but their steps quickly disappeared into the distance and left us alone, convulsing in that winter waterway.

'When consciousness began fading, we left the river, sensations dulled, bodies useless and shaking. We undressed, dried ourselves with snow, and began towards camp, knowing we would not survive long naked and exposed. Carrying soaked furs, we ran to the women, hoping for fire, dry clothes, weapons, and revenge. We found our campsite empty, its activities abandoned, and the fire smouldering. The men had killed my father and uncle to steal my mother, sister, cousin, and aunt.

'We nurtured the fire to life, dried our clothes, and slowly returned feeling. When dressed, we returned to the killing ground. My father and uncle lay mutilated and colourless in blood-soaked snows. The man my father killed remained, his family unable to take our women and him. We seized our spears and knives, and fell upon the men's tracks, blinded by hatred, disregarding our physical disadvantage, determined to butcher. But nightfall halted our chase and settled us inside a forest, silent beside a fire, our anger too horrific to voice. That night, snowfall washed away every track, ending our chances of seeing our family again. We were alone, my brother my only companion until a group accepted us four winters later.'

The couple lay together, quietly sharing sympathy and sadness. They watched shadows flicker across the fire-lit walls, both adrift in the past. The memory of his family tortured him, the women's fate a desperate curiosity without chance of resolution. Abandoning his father and uncle to die, and hiding while the women were abducted, shamed him. He hid from the disgrace, too upset by its accusations. He remembered instead being loved and being important to his family. That simple kindness had added worth to his life, a value lost when alone. But he missed his brother most, his loss was an agony undiminished by time, and his death impossible to confront.

He disguised his anguish behind impassiveness, understanding his stoicism gave her confidence in him and their future; he needed to seem unbreakable. He suppressed further reminiscence and guided himself towards less affecting thoughts. They turned the conversation towards more optimistic contemplations: raising a large family, having strong children to take care of them, and being grandparents. They were happy their firstborn would arrive at winter's end and have a summer to grow before the colds returned. She was nervous about mothering without family support but never doubted she would manage.

He promised her their next child would be born at the Settlement, protected by support and abundant food. His conviction possessed Mane with the same belief and made her excited for an end to hardship and deprivation.

Each night they sought each other as darkness settled, not needing words, their fondness and lying together enough comfort. The Wind God would whistle past their cave, sweeping the fire's smoke outside, still singing him to sleep despite his adulthood. Mane would lie in his arms, their shifting child holding their sleepy attentions, until they drifted away.

TEN

WINTER WAS OVER AND the Winter God had retreated to rest for his next invasion. The snows were gone, the days darkened later, the sun rose higher, and the winds chilled less. The world thawed gratefully, and life emerged from the softening earth. Winter had been kind, they had rarely been hungry, cold, or concerned by predators. They had grown devoted and holistically appreciative of each other.

He walked over brown dormant grass towards the Burning Red, carrying a boar around his shoulders, hungry and eager to eat with Mane. He knew he had softened in her company and become less impulsive, and he feared himself more vulnerable because viciousness won fights. But despite this, he was happier—no longer lonely and his thoughts less turbulent. He thought his transition natural, that men and women moulded into each other and moderated each other's harsher qualities.

Grey clouds were collecting overhead. He expected rain before nightfall, but welcomed it, finding it comforting. They could eat inside, dry and warm, serenaded by innumerable drops pounding rock, relaxed and satiated.

He approached the Burning Red, but found himself suddenly

uneasy. Without reason, apprehension crept over him, his calm dissolved and cold swept his skin. He slowed, each step indecisive. As he climbed into the cave, fevered female whines spilled from inside. He shivered, and his prey fell to the ground. Drenched in dread, he slowly entered. The scene was horrific.

Mane lay in cloudy blood, skin and hair sweat soaked, cheeks saliva flecked, eyes wide and devoid. She stared vacantly through him, pale and drawn. Shallow breaths rasped from white lips, each inhale an agonised sob. He fought surging alarm, striving for coherence. He knelt, unsure how to react, a powerless observer unable to intervene.

He crawled closer, dragging his knees into the blood. He lifted her clammy body to his chest and hugged her. She was oblivious and expressionless save her agony-lined face. In whispers he asked what had happened, but she did not respond, her lucidity was gone. She seemed disconnected from her body, her every sound the incoherent whimpers of delirium.

The world had collapsed into an unreal nightmare. How long had she suffered and struggled to stay alive, hoping he would return to save her and their child? But he was impotent, a useless spectator to her dying. He cradled her as her death throes grew infrequent and feebler, and he watched her unfocused eyes drift blindly. Mane was gone—he held a vacated body near death. He could not speak, he had not the coherence. He could only manage shock and transfixion as her breathing grew shallower.

Finally, she died, and he was alone. He felt nothing, his world had crumbled too quickly. He clung to her, thoughtless and numb. After a time, he laid her down and stared at her; her eyes and mouth open, her face contorted, dead by his child. Despite his detachment, she was difficult to bear. He pulled furs over her, trying to distance the distorted imitation. The girl that had given him contentment was gone. Their child, plans and future, were gone.

The cave became smothering and uncomfortable, pushing him

outside. He exited into sunset, stepped onto the grass, and managed a few steps before slumping against the mountain wall, a vacant creature without spirit. He was incredulous and adrift, unable to assimilate events.

Night's cold wrapped around him. He began shivering, but his detachment did not break. When the beginnings of rain touched his face, he barely noticed, nor did his reluctance to move lessen. When drops became rainfall and drenched him, he remained still, unable to reengage with the world.

He trembled in the wet and cold until finally shaking. He chastised himself, trying to force concern, grasping for the world left behind. Some instinct begged him to dry and warm himself, so he hauled himself up; his own weight seemingly increased, and his strength equally lessened.

He entered their cave and picked up Mane, keeping her face and pregnancy covered to distance the reality. He climbed outside and walked her into the trees. He left her deep in the forest, resolving never to venture near her remains again. He wanted to forget her final moments, afraid they would replace his memories of her.

When returned inside the cave, he built a fire and dried himself, and with the furs unnecessary for summer, he soaked up the blood and then abandoned them in the forest. He retrieved and carved the boar, then cooked it over the fire, trying through routine to reacquire some control. He turned the meat, slowly browning it, watching the rain as he cooked, feeling its melancholy echoing his loss.

When the food was ready, he had no hunger. The chores had distracted him, but he could not escape his damage. His appetite had withered, his energy gone and spirit dissolved. He strived for normalcy and chewed, hoping to reawaken hunger, but each mouthful was a struggle, so he put the meat aside.

Without tasks to distract him, he felt barren and uncomfortable, so he sought sleep to escape. He shut his eyes and hid inside the darkness, but found himself more unnerved. He writhed through this discomfort, sleep unreachable, his mind unbearable. He persisted seeking sleep, reluctant to return to the world, hoping dreams could temporarily spare him, but after much agonising, he abandoned trying.

He opened his eyes to a darkened cave; the fire was low and night had fallen. He felt numb and wanted this apathy to end. Outside, rain thrashed the sodden earth, and its song filled the cave. The Wind God howled and reached for his attention, imploring he escape the cave and all that was familiar. He could not manage objection, he had nothing here.

He would leave Mane, their life together, their dreams and future. He would fight to save himself; he would not be dragged into depression again. In another place, this present would become the past, and perhaps he would be freed.

The rain could not delay him; his resolve had hardened. He packed away the boar meat, a knife, furs, tinder, kindling, tools, bowls, and two spears, then without reflection, climbed through the entrance into the soaked outside. He bounded through the forest, between dark trees, fighting defeatist thoughts, fearing the loss of both Quiet and Mane had damaged him irrevocably. With Mane, he had rediscovered happiness, then had it ripped away; he doubted he could feel such affection again.

The rain poured through the treetop canopy and spilled from empty branches onto him. It found passage beneath his clothes and ran over his skin. He ignored it and marched on, feet churning mud, arms knocking aside obstacles; he would not eat or rest until his life with Mane was distant. The starless sky promised a relentless downpour, but he would not consider shelter. He needed new surroundings and no reminders of the past, and he had to exhaust himself—sleep would be impossible otherwise.

He stiffened against his shivering, bowed his head, and beat fanatically through the forest and rainfall, tensing against the cold, stubborn against the wind. He pulled his furs tight around himself, wet and shivering, feeling his discomfort somehow a penance for a transgression he could not identify. He felt contempt for his body crying for warmth; he deserved no respite. He strained to provoke anything besides resentment for the world, himself, and Mane. Full of bitterness and hate, he cursed everything and raged against the gods.

He pushed on, ignoring sense and the overrunning cold, concerned only with covering distance. With rising speed, he pushed the familiar forest behind and tore into unfamiliar territory, unwilling to exist near anything recognisable. His teeth clenched to stop their chattering, his back stiffened against shaking, and his thoughts stubbornly resisted measure. His home with Mane grew distant until finally he felt separated from his old life, allowing him to consider rest.

He trudged through the mud and rain until he found a large fallen tree lying angled to the ground, its base suspended by its roots. He climbed beneath it, evading the rain, and opened his pack to begin a fire. He found dry wood and built his hearth, packing it with bark from the trunk's underside. He coaxed smoke into the kindling and flame onto the tinder.

When the fire was prospering, he nestled by its heat to dry and warm himself. He retrieved some boar meat, determined to eat despite his lack of hunger. He chewed, but his efforts unsettled his stomach and irritated him. He persisted through the laborious process, finding it unpleasant and disheartening.

Overhead, the sky wept without sign of tiring, turning rains into storms, filling the world with its drumming. The clouds had darkened, threatening to rain all night. As the showers became torrential, lightning tore across the sky, igniting the dark. Thunder rocked the world and drowned every other sound.

As the thunder echoed and the rain lashed, he huddled near the fire, trying to avoid the cold and wet. But the wind whipped rain over him and his hearth, until finally his flames were extinguished. He tried reviving the fire, but soon his efforts were hopeless. The fireplace grew wet, and he soaked.

An ugly irritation consumed him, then an intoxicating overwhelming madness. Without control, a livid depression broke inside him and released dormant hate. The loathing was inescapable and consuming, extinguishing his reason. He seized up his belongings and fled into the storm, an unthinking feral animal tearing purposelessly through the undergrowth.

He had nothing but contempt for the world and everything living, for all the gods, for all their creations, and for himself. He wanted revenge on everyone and everything, to punish existence for its blind unfairness and cruelty.

Unable to channel his violence, his lunacy propelled him into a sprint. His kicked mud onto his furs, beard, hair, and face, but he barely noticed; he felt only mania. He did not care about anything anymore; life and death were indistinguishably malevolent. He scrambled across soaked earth, running with incoherent anger. Above, lightning illuminated the world, then cast it back into shadow, while the Thunder God screamed to serenade his mad surge into the unknown.

He ran unaware of expended time or covered distance until a chasm severed the land. He stopped on its verge and stared into the impenetrable black. Suddenly restrained, his body realised its exhaustion, and he sank to his knees, bent in the mud, chest heaving and struggling for air. His legs burned and head pounded, his body taken beyond its capability. The forest had cut and bled him, but he had not noticed.

He shut his eyes against the pain as the rain smeared his blood across his ripped skin. Lightning struck and thunder sang, bathing his world in light, igniting it like day. He slumped over the precipice and looked at the illuminated ground some thirty men's heights below.

While he lay gasping, some practicality surfaced; he could not continue like this. He knew some fissure in the cliff could house him while he warmed, and though he doubted himself capable of rest, he wanted to grasp for control. He ignored his mind's savagery and stood, striving for pragmatism.

He threw his belongings to the cliff floor and climbed down the jagged cliff face, rash and negligent, cutting himself further. He alighted onto the lower ground and began searching. A disobedient urge begged him to tear away again and purge his anger, but he fought himself and forced his search. He ignored the attacking rain and wind, burying his irritation, hiding from his quickly re-emerging violence.

Finally, and joylessly, he saw a large black cave cut into the grey cliff. He slowly approached, dreading being alone with his damaged self again. But as he neared, black shapes emerged from the cave. Four dark figures slowly prowled into the rain, skulking towards him, moving to surround him. Their yellow eyes beamed from their poised black bodies, their eagerness to kill him inconcealable. He watched the wolves stalk closer, unable to break his detachment, fear elusive. He recognised the mortal danger and knew apathy was endangering him, but he still could not rally concern. He searched for how he would have ordinarily responded, but he felt an uninvolved observer disconnected from his situation.

As the wolves crept near, he heard their low growls from behind clenched teeth and saw their heads lower, ready to pounce. He stared back coldly, unable to retreat, unlikely to survive. The heavy rain fell, and lightning speared across the sky, illuminating the four wolves and their bared teeth. The light died and the thunder crashed, and the wolves shifted closer, their attack only moments away. He held the lead wolf's eyes and challenged it.

'Let's begin this.'

As if understanding, the lead wolf leapt, jaws opening to tear him apart. Reflexively, he raised his spear and the wolf savagely seized it. As it tore into the spear, its feet clawed through his furs, opening cuts across his chest. He wrestled the wolf, but it drove him backwards and finally broke his spear into two shards. Wild terror suddenly seized him. His scream erupted, and he plunged his thumb deep into the wolf's eye. It howled in agony, abandoned the spear, and retreated into the darkness.

As the wolf escaped, two more charged him. He drove one of the shards into one of their heads, leaving it wriggling towards death. As the other wolf's teeth reached for him, he grabbed its throat, and held its bite from his face. The animal knocked him over, paws slashing his body, its jaws snapping for his neck. He closed his fingers around its throat and ripped away bone, hair, and flesh.

As the wolf writhed and died, the remaining wolf bit into his shoulder, shredding his muscle and skin. He dropped the dying wolf and thrashed against the bite. The teeth tore into him, striving to kill, but instead only ripping away his coat, freeing him from the struggle. The wolf immediately abandoned the fur and sought his face, but he shoved its dead brother between its jaws. As it bit into its brother, Follows smashed his fist into the wolf's head, driving it backwards. The wolf fixed him with hateful eyes, promising death, jaws bared and bloody.

Follows raised himself, his bloody left arm impotently hanging. The two adversaries watched each other, poised for the confrontation that would kill one of them. This time, Follows attacked first, launching forwards a moment before the wolf leapt. He seized the wolf's neck, lifted it from the ground, and hurtled it into the rockface. It kicked and thrashed, slashing and bloodying him further, but his rage disallowed him notice. He smashed its head into the cliff, and maniacally beat it against the rock, fanatic and vicious.

Finally, the wolf turned limp, and his shaking hand dropped its mangled body. He rolled manic, unfocused eyes over his surroundings, his mind lost to conflict's madness. His breaths rose like smoke in the dark and disappeared into the night, while the rain washed his sweat and blood onto the soaked ground. All the while, the world remained unchanged and unapologetic.

Despite his injuries and loss, he smiled a bloody grimace at the inexplicable forces which dictated his life. He had survived and defied the world. The Wind God whipped around him, witness to his resurrection, ally to his endeavours, guide to his spirit. Finally, he felt awake, his detachment and anger gone.

Amongst these feelings, he found understanding, and accepted the world's ways. The world was not unfair, it was just indifferent to the living, and there was no escaping its harshness. Everything ends, whether good or not. The grasses and trees blossom only to die in winter, like the infant born to inescapable death—their fates predetermined without consent. Somewhere in that tragedy was something consoling. Nothing could completely control its fate, so only misery could result from trying.

The only protection the living had against the future was the strength and flexibility to adapt. The only thing he could trust in this life or the next was his own strength, and strength was a choice. He had to struggle on against adversity to free himself, for there is no freedom if imprisoned by fear or burdened by tragedy. Realisation lifted and invigorated him.

'We must shoulder life's increasing weight and keep moving, taking into our future ever more of our past. We must carry our burdens without buckling, or we risk our spirit being forever crippled. We either rule our emotions or they rule us, even though our strength forever waivers. Sometimes we will emerge weaker, sometimes stronger; but how we continue determines our existence.'

He smiled with blood-stained teeth. He would suffer and be afraid again, but he was free. Tomorrow he would wake to the same sunrise that had watched over his ancestors and would watch over his descendants, the type of life he enjoyed under its gaze his choice. Cowards blame, the strong lumber on, scarred but free.

ELEVEN

HE WANDERED THROUGH THE cave's yawning entrance. Lightning struck and immersed the cave in light, revealing it twice the size of the Burning Red. Near the back of the cave, four wolf cubs walked precariously on weak legs, perhaps only thirty days old. They looked up at him, momentarily inquisitive, undaunted by his entrance, then they disregarded him, choosing instead to play. He left them alone and focused on making a fire to mend himself.

He ventured outside to collect enough firewood to last the night, then retrieved the three dead wolves, needing their furs to replace his shredded clothes. He built and ignited a fire, then placed a spearhead beside it. He removed his hacked and bloodied clothes and abandoned them into the soaked grounds outside.

Now his naked, slashed, and bruised body could reveal its damage. Long cuts streaked his body, spilling blood down his wet chest and legs, and some flesh had been severed from his shoulder. As the spearhead warmed, he stepped into the rain and cleaned his injuries, always preferring to burn them wet. Outside, the tempest raged, frenetically bellowing and pummelling the sopping earth, reminding the living they were not the world's masters.

He returned inside and judged the spearhead ready. He pushed its edge into his shoulder and singed it closed. Then he burnt his severest cuts, his experienced hands shaking from the pain. Cold sweats broke out, his teeth ground together, and tears of pain welled. He exhaled his agony in long breaths as the smell of burning flesh surrounded him, worsening his nausea. But eventually he finished, and the bleeding was stemmed. The pain would linger for days, but he would mend.

He washed again, naked against the rain, soothing his charred skin beneath the weeping heavens. He left the rains for the cave's fire and warmth. He sat beside the flames and began skinning the wolves, relaxed despite the aches and burning skin. He worked methodically, serenaded by rainfall, neither rushing nor dawdling. As his practised hands worked, his hunger emerged and stole his attention. He recovered boar meat from his pack and ate as he worked. He separated the furs and meat from their owners, then abandoned the bodies far from the cave. He scraped the furs of fat and tissue, then cleaned them in the rain. When finished, he positioned them around the fire to dry, planning to shape and stitch them after rest.

He lay by the fireside and pulled furs from his pack over himself. Overhead, the night cried without sign of tiring, its stars buried behind rainclouds. He watched shadows flicker upon the cave walls, and felt tiredness heavy his eyelids and limbs. The heavy rain was calming; a chorus of countless raindrops singing to him.

Nearby, the wolf cubs slept, pushed against the cave's furthest wall, evidently wary. He watched them, huddled together for comfort, their fates uncertain, fraught with difficulty and probable death. Like him, they were orphaned by circumstance, amends unforthcoming. They would likely die like his child, innocent victims of chance.

The thought of his child was difficult. Had fortune been kinder, he would now be a father and forever joined with Mane through parentage. Cruelty was woven into existence and punished without cause. He felt remorse for the cubs, but accepted their deaths, understanding the world's nature.

But now neither sadness nor the possibility of the injured wolf returning could deter sleep, he was drained and helpless against it. He would sleep with weapon to hand, ready to strike if disturbed, but he doubted the wolf would return. He lay, head sunk into furs, eyes listlessly wandering until they submitted and closed. He managed no further thought before sleep overtook him. The fire kept watch while the storm thundered on, but soon even the flames grew drowsy and retired. Stillness overcame the cave, tranquil into the morning.

Dawn coaxed him from sleep. He woke to overcast skies, finding the rain still falling but its vigour relaxed, the lightning and thunder exhausted. Rainfall resonated through the cave, the world solemn and serene. He looked outside at the grey sky, its darkness promising a day's rain. He sighed, rested but sombre. He decided against rising, content to watch the rain awhile.

His attention strayed to the wolf meat, noticing some was chewed. The wolf cubs had presumably braved theft before timidity provoked their retreat. Without raising his head, he tossed the nibbled meat to the cubs. The young wolves—lying abreast together—abandoned their dejection to investigate the meat. Finally, they concluded it safe and ate. He watched the inexperienced wolves tear weakly at the flesh, struggling, but eventually succeeding to wrest it apart. He saw the survivalism ingrained into the living, forcing their efforts; it was an irrepressible drive, forever resolute despite circumstances. He hoped they would drag each other to survival as he and his brother had done.

There was a comforting stillness surrounding him. From beneath his furs, he watched the rain thrumming the earth, his ears filled with its drumming. The deceased fire had left a blackened hearth and charred earth. Outside, the trees stood soaked, and plants bobbed in the rain. The surroundings were calming. He would gather for a fire, cook, and sew later, he wanted to lie with his thoughts.

A season of company made solitude strange; tolerating loneliness was a practised ability. Despite the Wind God's presence, he felt empty. He saw his god churning the rain and heard him swim around the cave, but he still felt alone. He had not spoken much with his god for a season, needing no insight, conversation, or assurance; but now he sought his answers, hopeful they would help him find solace.

'When I die, will I reunite with my family?' he asked the Wind God.

After a while, he felt the Wind God trickle answers into space.

'A person is a shadow of their spirit, limited by their body and mind. After life, you are freed from form, and able to exist everywhere. You are tied to everything, an eternal consciousness interwoven with every spirit. You will see those you have lost as they fully are, understand them better, and love them more deeply.'

The answer partly saddened Follows; he wanted reunion with the imperfect people he had lost. But knowing they lived on, and they would reunite, uplifted him.

His thoughts unavoidably wandered to Mane; her gentle company had given him the most contented time in his life. But despite his resistance, her dying moments asserted themselves above better memories. He strived to recollect their happier moments, but her death was irrepressible. He resignedly revisited her dying, believing its confrontation would weaken its impact and impression.

It was a wretched memory, but he bore it and slowly found something consoling. Death was permanent, and the living helpless against its permanency, but he held Quiet's and Mane's memory within him, defying the world's theft, keeping them in the world. Mane would join his brother in his thoughts, existing while he existed.

He noticed his own mind was bearable; an improvement upon yesterday. He still felt oppressive loss, but it was not overwhelming.

Mane's death had taken his happiness and left him lonelier than before he knew her, but he knew he could recover; his brother's death had taught him to endure. When Quiet had died, Follows had fallen apart, without desire to live and full of emptiness; but the Settlement and its divine Chief had reinvigorated his hope and distracted him with ambition, distanced him from misery, and diverted his energies while he healed. Slowly, time had strengthened him, until one day he found his load bearable. The Settlement would rescue him again.

The Settlement was half a season away. If he followed the stars, a coastline would soon interrupt the land. Then if he chased the rising sun's direction, he would find great mountains whose foothills led to the great group. The Settlement's noble people would welcome him into their group, where there was no hunger, where people lived peacefully without fear, deprivation, or conflict. The Settlement offered him rebirth as it had when Quiet died.

He lay contemplative and reminiscing, nostalgically drifting through the past. Hunger had surfaced and would soon send him into the rain for firewood, but he was unhurried, content to remain with his memories. He swam through his history, regretting and wishing to change much, but aware such desires were pointless.

Hindsight always exposed his foolishness. He remembered his old group and his ambition to succeed with them, and the resulting frustration when unsuccessful. But outside the group, objectivity was easier. The group's best women were already taken, and he and Quiet had always been regarded as outsiders, unlikely to ever establish themselves.

Though Follows always avoided confronting Quiet's death, a day never passed without thinking of him or missing his company and direction. To Mane he had been Wolf, independent and individual, but he was Follows and always would be.

He decided to prepare a fire and eat, but before he ventured into the rain, he wanted to record his lost life. He stood and painted a woman on the cave wall. When finished, he gave her a lion's mane, immortalising the girl forever. Beside Mane, he drew himself, scarred, bearded, and tall. The painted couple stood together, partnered, united again on the rock. He finished, happy with his mural.

He left the cave and strode into the rain.

TWELVE

THE SHOWER CONTINUED INTO the night, gently falling while he cooked, ate, and stitched. When finished, he fell asleep alongside the fire listening to the rain. Slowly, its urbane oration seduced him into dreams.

He woke to the dark blue preceding dawn, the heavens clear and tranquilly awaiting sunrise. He packed and left the cave, ambitious to exploit the day. Morning's cold enveloped him, the grounds soaked and winds cool. He walked into lifting shadows, guided by fading stars. The skies quickly brightened and filled with early birdsong. The sun peered over the horizon and chased away the remaining night.

During the morning, the Sun God heaved his light into the sky, washing him in sunshine and warming the wind. He was comfortable despite the recent days and still burning skin, his pace restrained but determined. He grazed on wolf meat without stopping, ignoring his recovering body asking for more rest. The horizons fell behind him as the sun arced through the sky, still weak but growing stronger.

As the Sun God summited, Follows found a river dividing the grasslands. He fished and ate on its banks, happy with his progress.

The sunshine and river guided him into brief sleep, against which he managed little resistance.

He rose under a falling sun and resumed. He conversed with the Wind God about his past, future, fears, and hopes, and praised the Sun God's resurrection and offensive against the Winter God. Under the easy weather and attentive company, he covered nine horizons before night fell.

As the Sun God withdrew, the Night God discoloured the heavens and freed the skies for Moon and star light. He settled inside a wood beneath an arched tree, watching the skies. He huddled beside a fire, fur-wrapped and tired, staring at the stars and Moon, ignoring earthly concerns and lost in thought. As the flames turned the firewood into embers, he fell into sleep.

The succeeding days imparted the same considerate weather interrupted only occasionally by cloud and light rains. He covered great distances under pleasant suns and slept peacefully each night, exhausted. Life emerged and coated the trees and ground, inviting more animals into the reviving lands. Hunting improved and hunger troubled him less, and the dark season's aches and stiffnesses disappeared.

While the world regrew, Follows covered much distance. He noticed his improving temperament and recovering mind, his strengthening nerves and spirit, his more optimistic and philosophical thoughts.

He revived old pastimes and drifted into contemplation and speculation. He began questioning emotion and finally concluded that it was externally absorbed. The rain and sunshine provoked differently, and each season stirred him incomparably. Death and birth moved him contrarily, and each object felt distinct. Like sound, feeling came from its source: burning's pain was absorbed from fire, cold was drunk from the winds and snows. A rock emanated a cold hardness, women inspired protectiveness, affection, and lust. Death released sadness, emptiness, and loss.

He felt the world was suddenly clearer and more beautiful—an endless reserve of stimuli—and realised how nuanced its provocations were. Men, women, animal, familiarity, appearance, and age all stimulated differently. He realised emotions must therefore also be impermanent, their potency and longevity dependent on the quantity ingested—like food. This was comforting, for pain and sorrow must therefore wane, and permanent detachment should be impossible inside such an emotion-saturated world.

He realised company always distracted him from self-reflection and contemplation, occupying him instead with relationship dynamics, hierarchy, responsibility, duty, respect, and allegiance. But alone he could live unreservedly and explore himself and existence; and though he feared solitude's emptiness, he believed its pain was distant.

Presently, he enjoyed being alone, grieved uninhibitedly, and gradually recaptured confidence. He exerted himself to exhaustion during the lengthening days and rested inside the temperate nights. Beside fires he watched stars climb the infinite darkness, imagining promising futures.

One morning, as the early sun rose through the empty heavens, his advance was arrested. He stood, subdued and enthralled, staring at the disappeared land. Brilliant endless seas filled the horizon—vast, shimmering, and exuding tranquillity. He had found the old man's foretold ocean and waypoint. The shoreline stretched towards the rising sun, showing him the path to the mountains bordering the Settlement.

The sea's beauty beckoned him closer and gladly he assented. He left the grass for the stony shore and stood at the edge of the ocean's reach. Sunshine scattered over the undulating surface, igniting the waves in brightness. He stared over the world's boundary, listening to the waves breaking over stones, smelling its distinct aroma, proud he had crossed the physical world in his lifetime. Follows trailed the coast, relaxed by the shimmering surf, emboldened that his destination was near.

He walked through the succeeding days within sight of the ocean, navigating prairies and intermittent woods. As the days grew longer, the nights grew more temperate, making his travel more comfortable and sleep under the stars frequent. The days passed easily, progress concerted and untroubled.

One clear morning, he saw a distant mountain piercing the horizon. Buoyed by expectation, he quickened his pace. During the day, a mountain range appeared, confirming he was proceeding correctly. Each day of his advance grew the mountains, until finally he arrived at their enormous foothills. He followed their lowlands, shadowed by their peaks. He entered into the tall pine woods covering the foothills and walked beneath their sun-speckled canopies, fishing and drinking their streams.

After two days, the evergreens tapered away into lush grasslands. Upon them, herds teemed and grazed, plants lined the streams, and fruit decorated the bushes. The land was uncommonly rich; this was clearly the Settlement's territory, its discovery now palpable. When he contoured up the mountain, the sea shone into view, filling the horizon with sparkling waves. The sight was captivating; he understood why the God Chief had built the Settlement here.

He journeyed onward, indulging in the surroundings, prey abundant and food diverse. He expected to imminently find people, provoking both his nervousness and excitement. His lonely days were dwindling, making him appreciate his concluding solitude. Days for thought and living his own schedule would become rare and privacy harder. He tried to ready for people, accepting he needed to be more accommodating and patient. There was anxiousness, but the potential awaiting him conquered his reservations.

He thought about establishing himself; he planned to learn the Settlement's practices, language, customs, and structures. He wanted to integrate fully, otherwise achieving influence and seniority was impossible. He would prove himself reliable, tenacious, and capable, earn respect and standing, obtain friends and allies, bolster his eligibility, partner well, and father his own large family.

Two days after entering the rich lands, he found signs of people. He found a fireplace, cold and burnt, sited on a rock bulging from the earth. Open plains surrounded it, confusing him, its placement reckless, without cover or protection. He examined it, wondering why they had taken such risk knowing it would have exposed them and drawn attention.

Slowly, his confusion faded as he realised the explanation. The fireplace's maker had been unafraid of attack or predators. They had believed there was no danger and had not considered defence or escape. The attitude was peculiar, but it communicated much. The Settlement controlled these lands and its people roamed them without fear.

He moved onwards, wondering what assurances allowed these people to discard caution, but gradually the Settlement's lands explained. There were no predators. He saw mammoth, rhino, auroch, bison, and deer, but nothing that could endanger people. The Settlement had driven away predators, presumably to protect themselves and prevent competition for meat.

Over the succeeding days, signs of human activity grew frequent: extinguished fireplaces, discarded animal remains, prints, and disturbed foliage. He saw paths so recurrently travelled that the ground was bare and hard. The people incautiously used familiar tracks, indifferent to predictability. The Settlement's lands were safe and precaution was unnecessary to survive; such an existence was an invigorating prospect.

He found deserted caves stocked with weapons and furs, their interior walls decorated in paintings and stories, some lately drawn. But the caves were empty, visited recently but rarely occupied. Their abandonment was strange until he realised them transitory lodgings for hunters needing replacement furs, weapons, and shelter. These caves divulged the people's organisation and thoughtfulness. The

Settlement required great resourcing, and the stocked caves ensured hunters could sustain their hunts no matter the circumstances. Impressed by the Settlement, his desire to join it grew enormously.

But presently he could not adopt the Settlement's blithe behaviour; their temperament and territorialism were still unknown. Where possible, he travelled through woods or near thickets, never far from camouflage. He trailed near manmade paths, hidden, vigilant, and guarded.

The day after discovering the stocked caves, he settled inside a copse overlooking some lowlands. He watched the blue night soak into the warm orange skies and rain crimson onto the grasslands, gradually inviting dusk. He reclined under twilight, listening to the quiet and watching its stillness. That evening he saw people.

As he drifted to sleep, a spark ruptured the dark. His tiredness disappeared and he focused upon it. It was a fire. He watched motionless as the flames grew into a blaze and threw visibility onto its surroundings. Around the hearth, people's shapes illuminated, each casting long shadows into the encircling gloom.

He was both excited and nervous, still disbelieving people would build such a blatant fire. The group was about four hundred paces away, without children, probably a hunting party. Around the flames, people cooked, talked, or lay to sleep. He counted thirteen adults, all relaxed and none on guard. He coveted their confidence, and hoped to soon be amongst them and perhaps find the companionship that had always eluded him.

When dawn rose, he would approach; contact at night was too dangerous, they would need time and visual forewarning to conclude him peaceful. In the morning the hunters could watch his approach and allow him to assess their hostility. Contact was dangerous, but the possibilities were worth the risk.

He tried to sleep, but anticipation made rest difficult. Instead, he watched the fire glitter in the dark and die to cinders before his cluttered emotions subsided and he slept.

THIRTEEN

HABIT ROUSED FOLLOWS BEFORE first light, opening his eyes to the night, its canopy adrift with stars and moonshine. He ate while the night faded, behind a broad deciduous trunk overlooking the dark lands below, waiting for the world to shed its shadow. Darkness slowly lifted and shapes began to surface. Before the sun could glimpse the horizon, dawn revealed the sleeping men.

The light prompted the men's rise. As light filled the aether, the thirteen shadows gradually exchanged their dark coats for detail. The men encircled an extinguished hearth, accompanied by the bones of last night's meal. He waited, delaying his approach to allow the men to fully wake and compose.

They rose leisurely and sleepily gathered their possessions. As they readied to depart, sunlight skimmed the horizon, scattering sunbeam shards through the skies, inviting colour into the dusk. Light poured onto the distant sea, flushing the waters in reflection. The morning was clear, and it was time to make contact.

He raised himself, breathed deeply, and stepped outside the trees. He descended the hill towards the men, his pace restrained despite his fear. He walked cautiously closer, fighting the urge to flee. He forced each step, eyes fixed upon the men, thoughts tense.

His walk was calm despite his fear; he wanted his approach to communicate peacefulness.

He reached for self-control, reminding himself that only a patient and accepting people could live amongst so many. Without tolerance, no group could accommodate people's incompatible characters and ambitions. Traits enabling stability, such as forbearance and consideration, would be encouraged, and violence discouraged. These people had tempered man's fractious loyalties and rivalries and united. He reasoned anyone raised in such an environment would grow patient and hospitable.

These thoughts helped him forward but could not make him abandon caution. Once noticed, he would stop far enough away to escape should he meet hostility. The men would either extend him gestures of peace or respond aggressively—he would respond accordingly.

He appreciated his age and sex were dangerous; they had provoked violence his entire life. Men prudently eliminated threats to protect themselves and their families. Everyone suspected outsiders; they possessed neither the loyalty nor shared interests of family, making contact dangerous and imprudent. Coexisting with strangers often caused tension and resentment, usually resulting in separation or violence. He would not assume the men ignorant of these truths and die blinded by naive dreams.

As he reached the hill's base, some men noticed him. Slowly, they abandoned readying and coalesced to watch him. Follows stopped, his chest thumping, his body shaking, equanimity lost. He watched the men, knowing they were discussing and assessing him, debating his intentions and their response.

Two hundred paces separated the men, their outlines silhouetted against early azure sky. He waited for their reaction, anxiety unsettling his stomach. He struggled to swallow, his throat dry and tight. He lingered in the discomfort, the wait insufferable.

Finally, after an excruciating time, the men responded. A lone man left the group and walked towards him, his pace slow and demeanour easy. The man carried a spear, but his intensions seemed peaceful: if the men intended him harm several would have approached. Coming alone was also unlikely a ruse, as it placed the man in unnecessary danger. The man was risking himself to invite trust and attempt contact, the spear was just insurance against Follows' unknown temperament—to encourage his cooperation and a final resort should he prove violent.

Relieved, Follows exhaled, elated the men had not responded aggressively. But despite their gesture, he remained vigilant. He held his spear, reassured by it, ready for violence should the stranger turn hostile. He watched the lone man cross their divide, his detail slowly emerging.

The man's hair was braided, brown, and clean. His furs were new, well-made, and well-fitted. He reckoned the man had seen twenty-six winters; his movements were easy and betrayed no injuries. He was a hand shorter than Follows, his build lean and fit, his skin tanned. The man was almost completely unscarred—strange for an adult male, his history evidently peaceful.

When the man was ten paces away, he stopped, his spear held loosely by his side to display his disinclination to use it. The man's beard was dark, his features and expression kind. Follows met the friendly eyes and saw the man's curiosity and nervousness. The unscarred stranger nodded, trying to communicate goodwill.

Follows returned the gesture, hiding his discomfort. His breathing was heavy, his limbs light. Despite the tension, Follows saw the unscarred stranger's fear. The stranger's eyes traipsed his scarred body, seeing his bloody past, making him regret their conference. Follows needed to relax the unscarred stranger.

Follows slowly laid his spear down. The unscarred stranger watched him, motionless, unconsciously poised, eyes fastened to Follows' every movement. Follows took his pack off and retrieved some meat from it. He offered it to the man, trying to earn his trust.

The unscarred stranger immediately relaxed. His face exchanged its apprehension for relief, and he smiled, his shoulders descending from readiness. The unscarred stranger walked closer and took the meat, gestured thankfully, and ate happily. The unscarred stranger's friendliness seemed genuine, calming Follows.

The unscarred stranger turned towards his group and waved, assuring them of his safety. The waiting men watched motionless, probably still nervous for their companion. The unscarred stranger returned his attention to Follows and gestured he return with him. The prospect of being helpless amongst so many frightened him. Outnumbered, he was defenceless, reliant on unknown men's mercy. He knew union was impossible without suffering this risk, but experience still begged he run.

But the prospect of revisiting loneliness persuaded him to chance the men. Without the Settlement, he was adrift without purpose, without an ambition to inspire. A directionless life was empty, and a meaningless life was pointless; he could not face such purposelessness. His hope defeated his caution, and he resigned himself to the risk. He collected up his possessions and stood, signalling his willingness to return with the unscarred stranger. Together, the men fell into a gentle amble across the lowlands.

They walked alongside, but he kept watching the unscarred stranger and the hunters, careful of treachery. When he neared beyond escape, he resigned himself to brutal defence should he be attacked—determined to kill as many as possible before he died. But he witnessed nothing suspicious, so he continued until only twenty paces from the group.

Then his legs seized, reluctant to venture him closer. Paralysed by vulnerability, his composure dissolved. He wavered indecisively, struggling for self-possession, dithering without tactic. He stared at the twelve silent men, each examining and curious. Despite his terror, he saw their unease, probably also disconcerted by his scars. He realised they needed proof of his friendliness.

With shaking hands, he reached into his pack and retrieved his last meats. He offered the food, appealing to their mercy and to pacify any hostility.

He saw the men immediately relax. Then they smiled and discarded their seriousness, and crossed the gap to accept his gift, nodding and smiling gratefully. They passed the meat amongst themselves and ate. Some men rummaged through their own possessions and offered him their meats, striving to broker a peace. He was surprised by their kindness and lack of reticence despite his foreignness; they were incautious and probably unused to danger.

A period of relief and uncertainty followed, the men relaxed but unsure how to proceed. To progress the proceedings, Follows stooped and drew people underneath horizontal lines in the dirt, trying to illustrate people beneath shelters. Though he knew nothing of their manmade shelters, he knew they must have some form of overhead cover.

The men watched him drawing and discussed amongst themselves, probably debating his meaning. Communication without language was a laboured process, but some understanding was usually established. As the number of people and coverings increased, the men finally understood him. They waved hands between themselves and his drawing, informing him that they were from the Settlement. Follows drew a final man underneath cover while pointing at himself, conveying his desire to join them.

The men nodded thoughtfully and conferred amongst themselves, their discourse unintelligible but inferable. He watched their expressions and listened for the emphases that universally inhabit dialogue and betray sentiments. He watched to whom the men directed their words and which men earned the most attention, enabling him to discern their leader. Those in charge rarely talked the most, but they were usually the most listened to. The unscarred stranger appeared to be the natural leader.

Follows was relieved by the familiar behaviours and dynamics;

these people were human despite their extraordinary home and divine Chief. He had feared finding people of ascended sentiency and being too primitive to integrate; but they were the same impermanent and fragile creatures as him, though their dispositions were unusual. Their humanity made his ambitions possible: to demonstrate his competence and secure respect, to earn standing and status, to win a desirable partner, and to grow a family.

While the men talked, he examined them, noticing them all similarly unscarred. The reason was obvious: these men did not fight, suffer predators, or endure harsh conditions. They hunted safely and resolved their disagreements peacefully. He felt reassured—his mistreatment was unlikely, and the men seemed incapable of ruthlessness.

He looked for a physical rival, a male instinct he believed as automatic as lust and competitiveness. Although the men were healthy and strong, some taller and broader, they lacked the robustness earned by many arduous seasons. The Settlement provided for its inhabitants without strenuous demand, a freedom he imagined made possible by their God Chief.

The men concluded their conversation and returned their attention to him. The unscarred stranger pointed at Follows, then a youthful man, then his diagram, indicating Follows accompany the young man to the Settlement. The young man had seen about sixteen winters and was the group's youngest, his beard thin wisps, his body not fully developed. The men were presumably conserving their stronger members for hunting, incautiously and naively trusting him with their colleague's safety.

The young man looked proud of his responsibility, obviously liked but impressionable and without influence. Follows involuntarily felt contempt for the youth's wish to please his peers. Follows' own reaction surprised himself and brought back memories of the judging and calculating behaviours encountered within a group, qualities forgotten about while alone. But he believed these behaviours unnecessary amongst fair people and endeavoured to restrain them. He would try to emulate the Settlement's nobility so he could ingratiate himself.

He conversed agreement with nods and smiles and exchanged farewells. He departed with his guide, made confident by the men's kind natures that their group must be stable, comfortable, and tolerant. But despite the men's kindness, he was still relieved to be away from them; he had become unaccustomed to crowds. The company had been draining and overloaded him. He had grown unused to people's complicatedness, nuances, and intentions; but he would relearn to handle groups in time.

Under a gracious climbing sun, they walked. The clear skies promised warmth, and within a horizon, the humidity cajoled the pair into any shade upon their path and to relish every passing breeze. They travelled in comfortable silence, immersed in their own thoughts, pausing beside each stream to drink and drench themselves. They rested occasionally in the shade, where he appreciated the surroundings and thought about the future.

He had never seen such rich lands, unmistakably cultivated by gods for their sibling on earth. He thanked the gods for guiding him here to live under a god's guardianship and amongst kind people. He vowed to integrate and discard his ruthlessness—such was unnecessary to survive now.

They walked through the day under the Sun God's heat, yet had still not arrived as the sun neared the horizon. The distance the hunters had travelled from home confused Follows. They had ignored herds and easy prey, making him question why they had journeyed so far. He was briefly disconcerted and feared deception, but slowly calmed himself. The men had ignored the best opportunity to kill him and earned no better advantage by ambushing him later. The men would also not have needlessly endangered their youngest companion. But he remained unsettled until he realised the men had not been hunting. He supposed they could have been collecting goods or patrolling, but either way the realisation calmed him.

The sun began fading and more comfortable temperatures intruded. They continued contentedly under violet-tinted skies, through reddening lands, watching the heavens pour colour; the godly displays mesmeric and affecting.

Follows' attentions lingered skywards until he stepped onto hard ground. The soft grass had disappeared and been replaced by hard dirt drubbed solid by countless footsteps. Like the earlier paths, the earth was bare, except here the entire area was barren. He was close to the Settlement; this ground was continuously used.

They continued up a hill, his nervousness mounting. Anxiously, Follows summited and saw the Settlement. Awe stilled and stupefied him, the scene without comparison, alien and vast. Below the hill, a hundred smoke trails escaped a hundred blazing fires, filling his vision with lights. The smoke melted together into scarlet clouds, streaking heavenward, while the fires spilled light onto their audiences, revealing hundreds resting, eating, playing, or talking; their numbers overwhelming. Amongst the people, there were hundreds of triangular structures, two men tall, their walls smooth, their shapes unnatural. He smelled cooking meat and fire smoke. Beside the Settlement wound a stream that drifted into the sea—shadowed, sanguine, and calm, its closeness comforting.

He stared, bewildered and awestricken by the Settlement's size and strangeness. He noticed his quick breathing, tense shoulders, and fear. He felt incompatible with the Settlement—too unsophisticated to assimilate and too ignorant to be useful. He was outlandish and incongruous, his ascent to seniority implausible. Weariness permeated him, all his travelling suddenly seeming wasteful and his dreams ridiculous.

But he fought these doubts, determined to stop fear chasing him away; he knew retreat would forever cause him shame and regret. He exhaled, reached for strength, and forced himself onwards.

The young man had waited patiently and understandingly, which Follows appreciated. Together, they sauntered down the hill into the Settlement, amongst the triangular structures, passing families singing, talking, and bathing in firelight. The structures were presumably shelters, but he wondered if they were constructed using divine means. He passed one and stroked his fingers across its smooth walls. He recognised it was bison skin, and realised they were manmade shelters. He felt comforted knowing he could learn how to construct them. Perhaps time could make him compatible with the Settlement after all.

He attracted stares, but he ignored them, wanting to escape the attention. Fortunately, the young man greeted people with only waves and pleasantries and avoided conversation. Follows knew his appearance and savaged body were disconcerting, but he thought this temporary. New beginnings allowed people to remake themselves, and he would adapt to the community and earn acceptance.

They continued along paths that twisted through the human enclaves until the young man stopped him outside a shelter. The young man pointed at himself and then the lodging, explaining it was his home. He then mimicked sleeping, communicating it was time to rest. Follows was relieved, eager for the dark and a refuge from people.

The young man pulled back a drape and invited him into his home. Follows entered the black silence, stepping onto furred floors. He moved to a sidewall and settled himself upon a fur, staring into the shadows above. He heard the young man rustling into comfort nearby, and felt fresh wind sweep around the enclosure, gusting from the shelter's perforated apex. The quiet provided him release from people and let him finally relax.

He felt his tension ease and tiredness assert itself. The company had exhausted him, and despite his cluttered thoughts, sleep was quickly claiming him. His eyes closed and his mind wandered, falling upon comforting memories. Before sleep arrived, he thought of Mane and their life together. He remembered wishing for the Settlement even when with her, even when content. This made him suspect he could not appreciate his present without dreaming of the future and that perhaps he was incapable of achieving contentment.

Inside the shadows, he relived his time with Mane, coveting each memory, pining for her, until finally fatigue overpowered him and he subsided.

FOURTEEN

HIDDEN FROM DAWN'S LIGHT, Follows slept until the young man nudged him from sleep, waking him to the shelter's humid dark. As his grogginess subsided, the young man pulled aside the shelter's entranceway, pouring early light over him. Follows squinted under the brightness and blearily rose.

He stepped outside into the morning and stretched away night's stiffnesses. He surveyed the Settlement, surrounded by the hum of conversation as people began their days. The shelters shone under young sunlight, almost beautiful, moderating the unease their strangeness inspired.

As he looked around, the young man gestured to him, stealing his attention, inviting Follows to sit with him at a nearby fireplace. As the men sat down together, the young man began drawing in the blackened ground. He drew two open-mouthed men facing each other, and then a line from one man's mouth to the other's ear. Follows understood the drawing was a conversation but was unsure of its meaning. The young man pointed at the speaking man, and then at Follows, explaining that he was the speaking man. The young man then pointed at the listening man, and then at the Settlement, explaining the Settlement was the listening man.

Follows understood; he was to speak to people. The purpose was surmisable: to accustom people to him, and possibly to locate people speaking his language. However, he believed the exercise pointless, the origins of his languages were too distant to encounter fellow speakers. But without words to argue, and desiring to see the Settlement, he nodded agreement. The young man seemed pleased. He stood and invited Follows to accompany him.

During the morning, he was introduced to people, but predictably, he was not understood. The interaction made him feel tense and smothered. His vulnerability proved impossible to ignore, making him defensive, nervous, and awkward. He could not stop analysing each situation for threats, responses, and escape. He strived to suppress his discomfort, attempting to trust, trying to accept his defencelessness.

Despite his distress and worry, the Settlement was still fascinating. Families built their shelters around a communal fireplace and area. Together the sprawling collection of family enclaves amassed into the Settlement, giving it a familial atmosphere. In loquacious groups amongst the shelters, women constructed knives, spears, and clothes, while others minded infants and children. The men were few, presumably employed outside of the Settlement. Company with the women was difficult. Unused to their company, indifference was impossible. He greeted them briefly, eager to escape.

Beside the Settlement, a river supplied water to drink and bathe. Across the river was a smaller collection of shelters. He thought these peculiar, as there was space to site all the shelters together.

He saw returning men and women carrying food and materials. The women—usually accompanied by older children—brought back hares, game, fruits, nuts, roots, vegetables, plants, and eggs. The men returned carrying furs, stone, fish, wood, and meats. The Settlement's practices were similar to his last group, differing only in scale and sophistication.

They walked to a lake on the Settlement's outskirts that was surrounded by green banks and hills. Men and women relaxed near the shore, probably resting between chores. When he saw children playing in the deep water, he was stunned. He watched them swimming, captivated and puzzled by their buoyancy, trying to determine how they floated. Coveting their ability, he resolved to learn it.

They met many people but no fellow speaker. He assumed the people they approached were foreign born since natives would know only their language. The quantity of foreign born demonstrated the Settlement's inclusiveness, but this confused him. He did not understand why the Settlement did not protect its land, nor why they shared it. The natives did not benefit, they lost territory, and were required to share their resources with unrelated people. Further, without familial and group loyalties cohesiveness disintegrated, undermining stability. He thought awhile about this and concluded that newcomers probably abandoned their tribal loyalties and ways. This seemed a fair exchange for residency, otherwise tribalism would escalate into conflict.

The men followed the worn paths streaking through the shelters until the Settlement fell behind. The rich country surged around them, rustling in light winds. The sound was relaxing, reacquainting him with the familiar. He listened to it bristling overhead, feeling instantly more comfortable. The Settlement was severed from the wilderness' sounds, and filled instead with the noise of people, disallowing him the sounds he had grown around. He suspected he would never find the wilderness' peace amongst so many people.

He walked, enjoying the surroundings, until the trees and grasses began melting away. They were approaching the sea, its ardent blue appearing through the disappearing green. They alighted onto the white shore patrolling the sea, each step sinking into warm sands. As they neared the breaking waves, he stalled, staggered by the spectacle upon the sea.

Half a horizon away, black shapes drifted over the sea, and upon them sat men. He watched them float across the waves—black silhouettes against teal sky. Their activity was unfathomable, and the instrument of their travel inconceivable. He stood, awestruck and incredulous, again feeling inadequate and simple, but full of desire to join the men and share their experience.

He watched until suddenly distracted from his astonishment by the young man smiling, obviously amused by his amazement. He felt his primitiveness was being mocked and was angry at the condescension. He hated being read, preferring the advantages afforded by being less predictable. But his surprise had been too sudden to disguise, and he admonished himself. He turned to the young man, wanting to punish him, but knowing this would result in banishment or maltreatment. Behaviour had to be controlled to coexist with people, otherwise trust and cooperation were impossible.

His incensed expression shocked the young man and killed his smile. The young man's eyes fell downward, realising he had insulted, suddenly afraid and apologetic. Follows saw the remorse and immediately lost his anger and regretted his temper. He wanted to forget the incident and continue amicably.

Cordially, Follows gestured they continue, and they departed along the beach together. He kept turning to the seafaring men, unable to ignore his fascination. His desire to join the men was a powerful attraction, both alluring and intimidating. He remained captivated as they walked along the warm sands until he noticed a group of men working further up the beach.

The four men were pouring concentration upon a downed tree, two men in length, half-a-man thick. The men were hacking and scraping shavings from the trunk's innards, inferably constructing the vessel that carried people across the sea.

The young man took Follows to the men and greeted them jovially, evidently friends. Follows was encouraged to speak but was not understood. He supposed most newcomers originated from nearby, making encountering shared languages common. Perhaps locating a fellow speaker was standard practice, as it provided tutors to hasten learning. He waited while the young man talked, examining the seagoing hollow tree that somehow stayed afloat, unsure how something so heavy did not sink.

Eventually they left the men and continued along the beach, surrounded by sea-laden breezes and sea-scattered sunshine. They occasionally waylaid more men to test his language. Each attempt was unsuccessful, but he was indifferent, content to remain near the whirr of surf over sand. The sea had never surrendered its influence, and still evoked memories of his youth and their first encounter. Its charm was indefinable, but it reminded him of the gods' power, quieting his restlessness, and provoking self-reflection and perspective. Once settled into the Settlement, he would push to go to sea; he wanted to ride the divine border and experience something otherworldly.

He was so absorbed in thought that he barely noticed the recognisable words. Surprised, he turned towards their speaker. An old man sat astride a rock under the shade, his frame thin, his hair and beard plaited, long, wavy, and white. His decrepit appearance shocked Follows: he had never seen a body so worn and broken.

Initially, he assumed the man was deformed and sick, but he quickly realised an age beyond his experience was responsible. The face was wizened and tanned, his eyes narrowed by sagging eyelids, eyebrows overgrown and white. The old man's cracked hands held a staff for support, his body enfeebled—punished by time, robbed of strength and future. He was mesmerising, an example of everyone's fate if alive long enough.

Outside the Settlement, such age was impossible. The winters, starvation, rivals, and injury killed the weak. When the old slowed down the young, they were left behind. When they could not forage and hunt, they starved. The young subsidised the old, but in lean times only the strong survived. Without the Settlement's insulation and generosity, the old man would have been long dead. Presumably the old were exempt from contribution and self-sufficiency, evidencing the community's charity and abundant food.

Meeting the old man's gaze, Follows spoke.

'How many winters have you seen, old man?'

The old man chuckled, his smile worn and eyes mischievous.

'You carry no airs. You're a wild one. I've seen almost seventy winters, my young friend. Which is more than you'll see with your manners.'

The old man seemed to enjoy teasing. Follows liked the old man despite being mocked, and hearing the familiar language was cheering. It was his old group's language; he had never expected to hear it again.

'How do you know this language, old man?' Follows asked.

Again, the old man laughed.

'You are brusque, wild one. No time for niceties? My woman and I left the group that speaks our language over forty winters ago. When she died, I never thought I'd hear it again, life never fails to surprise. But a shame I have to revive my old language with a headstrong man instead of a pretty young woman.'

Follows was disconcerted by the disrespect, and feared it might spread to others, for humans are social creatures, and attitudes are consequently infectious. He examined his conduct, wondering if his manner was inviting insolence. He acted naturally, but his inexperience of humans made perspective difficult. His adolescence had been spent solely with his brother and his recent seasons almost completely alone. He recognised he was direct—he remembered how few from his last group had warmed to him. He had not been discourteous and was unsure how to behave to elicit respect. He had witnessed men ridiculing each other before, supposedly in jest, but he had seen only assertions of dominance. The fact that those most respected were the least taunted was no coincidence; so he avoided and was intolerant of teasing. He had to insist on respect without damaging relations—the old man was useful for both his language and knowledge.

'You criticise easily. Have you a problem with me?' Follows said.

The old man resignedly shook his head, his smile unchanged.

'Young men are so full of pride and quick to anger,' the old man merrily remarked. 'How can you bear your own company when your world is so serious, wild one?'

The situation felt peculiar, Follows had no means of demanding civility and was forced to bear the impudence to protect the Settlement's harmony. He had seen similar situations at his previous group when people insulted others, confident that they faced no retribution, knowing the group's disapproval of violence was sufficient protection. It was an aspect of coexisting with people he regarded as detrimental to dignity and self-regard, but he nonetheless persevered against the old man.

'If you behave civilly, old man, we might assist each other. I need your help with the language and understanding the Settlement. In exchange, I will help you with the tasks your age disallows.'

The old man nodded gently, his expression reconciliatory.

'I can't accuse you of timidity, wild one,' the old man said. 'I meant only for friendly exchange, do not worry over my manner.'

The old man began talking with the young man, giving Follows pause for relief that he had peacefully corrected his treatment. He watched the men's conversation and surmised it concerned his arrangements. When the men concluded their discussion, the old man spoke to him.

'My name is Salt. They call me such because of my long association with the sea. I am the head fisherman here. I'd like you to come live with me, mostly so I can take advantage of your youth, but I just might teach you somethings as well. Sound like an acceptable arrangement?'

'It does,' Follows responded.

'Good. Well come sit and listen to me ramble awhile, and if you're so inclined, you might learn something too.'

Salt waved away the young man, who nodded appreciatively

and departed down the beach. Follows settled himself on a rock beside the old man, facing the shimmering sea, content to sit and listen to the ancient man. As the day aged and dimmed, the two men remained together, talking, watching the daylight's hues slowly change and tinge the waters in richer colours.

Salt organised and coordinated the Settlement's fishing. He claimed a lifetime's experience let him predict the coming weather and read the sea's mood. With such age, Follows believed him. The old man was kind and unable to remain serious—prone to joking and difficult to dislike.

They talked through evening's shifting shades until the red sun plunged into the sea, scattering vermillion light across the darkening waters and encouraging them to return to the Settlement. They walked to Salt's home still in conversation, dyed by the last vestiges of sunlight, no longer strangers and pleased with their new company.

They left the cool sands for the hard-worn paths, surrounded on all sides by shadowed trees and fallen night. The light slowly extinguished and left the men traipsing through blackness towards their home.

FIFTEEN

DURING THE NEXT FEW days, Follows began hunting with the men, and learning from Salt about the Settlement's history, people, and practices. He listened to stories about its once warlike nature and people, disbelieving they were ever capable of much violence. The rich lands had tempted many differing and conflicting peoples into its luxury and plunged them into rivalry, burying generations in war. Slowly the groups were whittled away until one remained—the people belonging to the Chief's ancestors. Their group would become the Settlement, and the Chief's lineage its leaders. After generations of fighting, people were finally freed to live peacefully and to rue their forbears' brutality.

The Settlement's men were predominantly hunters. When they killed an animal, some men returned to distribute its meat and furs; the remaining men continued hunting until low numbers necessitated their return. The returning men's families had some priority over what was returned, but most was distributed amongst the community.

Men collected the furs, wood, and stone for the tools and shelters, and when predators were sighted, they formed patrols to track and kill them. The men prioritised the elimination of predators to reduce competition for food and make the area safer. Hunting outposts were scattered throughout the Settlement's lands in any cave that could accommodate provisions. The caves enabled uninterrupted hunting, providing places to rest, and replacement weapons and furs if needed.

The men were also fisherman, requiring them to be capable swimmers. Fishing and hunting responsibilities were mostly determined by preference and specialisation, though sometimes low resources dictated duties.

The women had their obligations: acquiring food; caring for children; scouring furs; making clothes, tools, and weapons; and assisting the elderly and pregnant. The women intimately knew the local area and gathered plants, fruits, and vegetables, and set traps for smaller game to diversify the community's food.

Each evening, as the sun retreated and the light faded, the Settlement abandoned work for the company of family and friends. They ate around campfires, talking, singing, debating, telling stories, and reliving memories. The old usually regaled the young with stories while the men and women cooked. People would eat and socialise until tiredness ushered them to their shelters and left the communal areas empty.

The community engaged in many games: sprinting, spear throwing, tests of strength, and swimming; but nothing earned more interest than wrestling. Only adult males fought, achieving victory through forcing their opponent to submit. Regular tournaments elected a champion—currently a man named Bear. Wrestling also provided an outlet for enemies to fight and rivalries to be settled so fatal violence in the Settlement could be avoided.

Men used wrestling to demonstrate their strength, to attract women's attention, and to earn respect. But it was the prospect of improving his regard which attracted Follows' interest: the sport was an obvious means of improving his renown amongst both the men and the women. He carefully watched the fights, learning and assessing, confident that in time he could beat most men.

The partnering of men and women was a simple ritual. At sexual maturity, a girl and her parents discussed the men she would consider. A young girl was sometimes too inexperienced to recognise the male qualities that would determine the comfort she and her offspring would enjoy, necessitating parental counsel. Sometimes a young girl's selection was predominantly physical, overambitious, or reckless, requiring parental intervention to protect her feelings and future.

The failure to pair a girl with a reliable male damaged the girl's life. If a man was a poor provider, or the couple separated, the girl's family assumed responsibility for her and her children, straining the family's resources. Once a girl had children, her prospects were few, as men wanted to invest in their own offspring, leaving her dependent on family.

Once a man was selected, the father approached him to ascertain his interest and to agree arrangements, freeing the girl from facing rejection and embarrassment. Once assurances were provided—and the families agreed the union sagacious—the couple began their adult lives together. The responsibility to protect and provide passed to the girl's partner, but both families—now united by the bond—imparted support.

Follows immersed himself in the Settlement, dedicated to integrating. Whenever an opportunity arose to impress during hunts or labour, he invested himself, using the endurance and skill earned by many seasons of independence and struggle. After fifteen days, he began feeling secure in the community, grasping its dynamics and behaviour. The only aspect he felt ignorant about was the God Chief, having not encountered him yet.

He had seen the God Chief's home, separated from the Settlement by two hundred paces, larger and more elaborate than normal shelters. Around the Chief's home were the shelters of his eight partners and offspring, all encircling a hearth, like other families. The Chief had little reason to venture into the Settlement—he and his women were provided for. When the senior administrators needed him to settle disputes and issues, they visited him.

But twenty days into his residency, Follows saw the God Chief wander into the Settlement to tell a story. Hundreds had amassed around a huge fire while the God Chief acted through his parable, flamboyantly spellbinding his audience. Follows could not understand the Chief, but he was still captivated. The Chief exuded presence, his dramatic movements mesmerising, his arms exaggeratedly sweeping with his story, serenading his words with drama. Follows watched the god's animation and energy, his long braided hair swaying wildly to his storytelling, spilling vigour, enchanting everyone.

The God Chief's body was inhuman and starkly contrasted mortal men. He had an abnormally large stomach and his limbs lacked muscle. He realised this god had constructed a body different from humans, but one presumably capable of tasks impossible for men.

The sweltering fire discoloured the heavens of stars, leaving an empty night sky above the enrapt Settlement. As the Chief danced through his story, Follows felt absolute authority radiate from him, demanding admiration, asserting his headship a birthright. The congregation was grateful for the Chief's company, their devotion mounting as it latened, infecting him with their reverence. Only the Wind God dared disturb the stillness, fluttering the scorching fire, brushing the audience, momentarily distracting him.

Follows' attention briefly shifted and fell upon an indifferent and disconnected old man. The old man's apathy starkly contrasted the enamoured senior men and women he sat with, stealing Follows' concentration. It was the Head Hunter, Hare. Hare coordinated the Settlement's hunting, a serious and respected man. He had been named Hare when young for presenting a hare to the adults and claiming to have caught it on foot. The audacious claim had earned him his lifelong name.

Hare projected authority despite his small size and advanced age. He had seen around fifty-five winters, his hair and beard long and grey; his youthful muscle was gone, but his sturdiness remained. He was objective, thoughtful, and systematic, his voice confident and persuading. Hare's seriousness prevented easy friendship, but respecting him was easy.

Follows found Hare's disinterest both curious and provocative. He bore the Chief's story neither insolently nor respectfully, his mind elsewhere, unconcerned with the performance or flattery. Hare's detachment broke Follows' captivation and stranded him alone amongst mesmerised people. Returned from entrancement, all the excitement and adulation seemed suddenly outlandish. Everyone was consumed beneath the crowd, infected by each other's adulation, their selves surrendered. Except Hare. He waited away the evening, free from influence, bored. Hare did not fear or respect the God Chief—he tolerated him; his attendance was a formality grown tiresome.

As the Chief conducted the audience, Hare looked on, unimpressed by divinity, his attitude like a father of a restless child. Hare was second to the Chief and his principal adviser, making Follows realise the Chief was not all knowing. The Chief's human form restricted his abilities and disallowed him omnipresence and omniscience. Realising the Chief was imperfect upset Follows' confidence in his leadership.

Follows stood between doubt and thought as the Chief concluded his story, bid farewell, and disappeared into the dark, escorted by Hare and the other senior men and women. Follows returned to his shelter rattled by insecurity. He had been inspired by the Chief and felt his power, but now questioned his experience, and doubted whether his reverence was deserved. Unconditional devotion to the Chief suddenly felt difficult.

As Follows roved underneath the dark sky and white stars, wrapped in the summer night's warmth, he found himself wanting to wander awhile. People streamed from the gathering into their shelters, eager for rest ahead of their tomorrows, leaving him strolling along silent passageways, listening to the wind swim around the Settlement. He became alone, a rarity in the Settlement, but welcome—he needed time with himself and his thoughts.

When only his footsteps upset the quiet, he felt calm and freed from people. During his residency he had immersed himself in the Settlement and lost time alone, leaving him feeling estranged from himself. The Settlement worked more than his previous group; the large number of dependents required it. Outside the Settlement, the inflexible world killed the weak, leaving those remaining fewer duties, and more leisure during undemanding periods. These easy times had been his happiest and sacrificing them to work for others seemed a heavy penalty.

He suspected overworking weakened relationships by limiting the time to grow closer and develop together. He also reckoned it smothered individual thought and growth. He remembered relaxing with his brother without task, talking and debating, building dreams and theories. Such reflection let him evaluate his wants and direction, and recognise the pointless. Without reflection, behaviour was not steered by thought, making people automatic instead of autonomous, which slowly stole purpose from existence.

He believed the Settlement's people were too busy for introspection. Unending tasks and interaction distracted them from insight and prevented them from discovering purpose and developing. Their characters became moulded by their surroundings instead of contemplation and consideration, limiting their imaginations and consciousness.

But he argued himself into accepting the Settlement's ways, recognising he would become old and require the care of others. He was unsure whether sacrificing his youth to extend his old age was sensible, but his opinion was irrelevant if he stayed—contribution was mandatory. Follows saw that no system could provide both lifelong security and personal freedom; he had to choose one.

He liked the Settlement. The people were kind, trustworthy, and friendly. He felt safe and no longer feared deprivation, predators, humans, or the weather. But he also felt congested and rushed. His resting and meals had to coincide with schedules, and finding time alone was difficult. The transition from isolation to company had been stressful. His feelings and thoughts felt more disconnected and his naturalness suppressed. He hoped these feelings were impermanent and that integration and friends would lessen his discomfort. Perhaps when partnered and a father, he would feel the Settlement was home.

He sighed, saddened by contentment's elusiveness. He slowly walked through the Settlement until its shelters fell behind. He stopped at the wilderness's border and looked into the dark world beyond. The trees were black silhouettes intruding into the night sky, their windswept branches rustling soothingly. His friend the Wind God was always nearby. He was forever watching, understanding, and sympathetic of his troubles. Their many seasons together had intimately acquainted them, making each expert at reading the other. Follows felt blessed by the company and unsure how he would have coped without their companionship.

He listened to his god move through the wilderness, creaking boughs and swaying leaves, seducing him into calm. He heard the whispers inviting him to leave but refused their invitation. He suppressed his impulse to escape, trying to remember the wilderness's loneliness, austerity, and danger, but instead he felt nostalgia. He knew humans coloured their pasts, forgetting the extent of their sufferings and revering their better times; he supposed it helped them cope.

He tried to remember his past without distortion, recalling the introversion, hardship, and desperation. He tried to persuade himself the Settlement was his best chance of a promising future, but these efforts made him realise he was forcing his feelings, that he was afraid to chance another life. This made him feel like a coward. But he would not flee the Settlement yet. He would trial the Settlement a winter and a summer, and then if still dissatisfied, he would take a woman and leave.

He turned from the dark lands and wandered along the empty labyrinth of paths towards Salt's shelter; it was late, and tomorrow's hunt was early. He arrived and lifted the entranceway and entered the darkness. He crossed softly to his area and settled amongst his furs, careful not to disturb Salt. He shut his eyes and let his body slacken and discard the day's tensions. But as he drifted towards sleep, Salt's voice rose from the shelter's recesses.

'Did you see our god, Wild One?' asked the old voice.

Wild One had become his name in the Settlement. He still thought of himself as Follows, but was indifferent, conceding his new name was relatively accurate.

'I saw him, old man,' he replied tiredly, his words tinged with disinterest to discourage conversation.

'Did our Chief's divinity impress you?'

The old man's irreverence was not unusual, but Follows noticed a probing inquisitiveness. Intrigued by Salt's curiosity, he replied seriously.

'I saw the natural confidence of someone who has never failed. He had no facade; he knew himself superior. I have known none like him. Everyone is humbled by survival and failure, and quickly learns their limits and fragility. But he possessed neither the bravado of the insecure nor the humility of the experienced. Only a god could be so.'

His words disappeared into the dark, but no reply followed. Follows ignored his irritation at Salt and turned into his bedding. But as he began towards sleep, Salt again disturbed him.

'I always thought my own children special, Wild One. With my unmerited praise, they grew with unfounded confidence. They developed characters typical of the successful, and applied themselves to endeavours beyond their capabilities, always believing themselves deserving. Sometimes some undeserved praise can founder the self-deception necessary to succeed.'

Salt's thinly disguised scepticism of the Chief's divinity caused silence. Follows was unsure how to respond, shocked Salt doubted the Chief so openly. He let the conversation die, wanting to collect his thoughts.

After a time, he wondered whether the Chief's divinity mattered. The people had confidence in the Chief's governance. Losing that could cause instability and leadership challenges, fracturing the group and killing people. If the Chief was mortal, then deception was less damaging than truth. Despite this, he decided truth was preferential; lies imprisoned people and distorted their views and reality. Follows did not doubt the Chief's divinity, though after tonight he did know the Chief's power and knowledge were limited.

He fought further contemplation, deciding his situation unchanged. He roved his memories for escapist thoughts, trying to distance himself from people's complicatedness.

His eyes instinctively looked towards the stars but met the ceiling. He lay staring into the darkness, mind wandering. For reasons he cared not to investigate, memories of his brother and their explorations together appeared and captured him. The boy and man that had protected him into adulthood did not desert him, even in death. Quiet was carved into his memory, and their past stained into his dreams.

Behind closed eyes, he and Quiet revisited their time together. They travelled his drifting consciousness, speaking unreservedly, playing, and relaxing as they had. They kept company until they wandered into sleep, and Follows was left alone again.

SIXTEEN

CALM BLUE SKY FLOODED with summer sun stretched into the horizon. Bright white clouds drifted slowly, the air warmly cloaking him and his companions. Deep green grass softened each step, combining with the weather to relax him.

He was three days into his hunt, but the weather had provided him a congenial excursion absent of difficulty. The nights did not require fire, or even cover, to provide him uninterrupted sleep. He had arrived in the Settlement some eighty days ago, and he reckoned the current weather the most hospitable so far.

He and four other hunters were stealthily crawling up a gradual grass hill, keeping hidden from the aurochs beyond, moving into a position to intercept them. The other half of his hunting party had flanked the aurochs, intending to drive them into his group's ambush. Unfortunately, the other men had poorly timed their attack, sending the herd towards them too early, beyond reach of their spears.

Follows and the men summited the hill in time to see their prey charging away. They resignedly watched, each man accepting their hunt prolonged. Had the weather been less agreeable, Follows might have been irritated, but the conditions disallowed such. He supposed later, his good mood had lessened his reserve and encouraged his attack. The herd were some three hundred paces away, but he decided to chance the improbable, and ferociously launched his spear at the aurochs.

A surprised laugh erupted from the men, but it died as their eyes followed his spear, realising it might reach. The spear plummeted down into the neck of an aurochs and crashed it into the ground. He doubted a further hundred attempts could have repeated the success, but that did not stop the men cheering.

He strode down the hill towards his kill, bashfully accepting the men's verbal and physical praise. His feat even provoked small competition amongst the men, who strived to throw their spears the same distance. The men playfully competed, but Follows knew rivalry always underlay competition. It was reassuring to observe men behaving familiarly.

He hoped his achievement would increase his renown. Ability earned admiration and respect, which raised status. Status improved chances to influence, and influence gave the ability to manipulate to one's advantage. He knew high-status individuals received disproportionate praise, but the only way to climb to that position was success. Hierarchy was a merciless but motivating battleground.

He listened to the men talk, understanding most of their conversation. He had been immersed in their language, and had diligently studied it, but felt uncompelled to talk, happy to just enjoy the weather and his achievement.

He saw the other half of their hunting party emerge over another hill in pursuit of the disappearing herd. They would continue to hunt while his party returned meat to the Settlement; the routine needed no communication.

The sun warmed his bare skin and kneaded his shoulders; light breezes touched him and carried through his hair. He felt relaxed and free from the stress of adapting to the Settlement. The men seemed to accept him and even respect him, which made him grateful and cheerful. His concerns fell away, and he drifted into thoughtlessness.

His hill gradually levelled into flatland bordered by other hills and woodland. He watched his surroundings—coloured by flowers and greenery, sun-reflecting and serene. He drifted disconnectedly, rooted in the present, without thought for the future or the past, until his trance was disturbed.

Movement from a nearby woodland broke his detachment and focused him upon it. Five dark silhouettes emerged from the trees, coalescing together under shade. They were three hundred paces away, each holding spears, still and watching. Follows saw his companions notice the men, yet they continued talking without concern. Neither the strangers nor his companions waved, or acknowledged each other, making clear they were rival groups.

Follows' peace was shattered, his aggression rose, and his body instinctively tensed and readied for conflict. He had never experienced such a situation without subsequent violence, and the memories of those encounters filled him with murder.

He studied his surroundings, looking for ambushes and ways to exploit the land to better kill the men. His viciousness and resolve hardened, ready to slaughter. He stared at the men, waiting for their advance, waiting for the killing to begin.

But the other men remained still, and his companions continued devoid of alarm. He was confused, unsure why the groups failed to react appropriately despite being rivals. He kept his eyes upon the other men, expecting imminent violence, but although the other men were trying to intimidate them, neither side moved towards conflict.

As they arrived at his kill, one of the men noticed his disquiet.

'Ignore them, Wild One, they won't harm us, they're just the Others from across the river. They were probably hunting the same herd, and they're annoyed we've deprived them.'

His companions began carving the aurochs, but Follows remained standing inside an ugly silence, unable to disengage, incensed by his companions' flippant attitude to these men. He remembered Salt's story of them.

They had arrived a generation ago, a whole group wanting to live in the Settlement's rich lands. They had settled across the river from the Settlement, kept their own language, beliefs, and rituals. They rarely mixed and believed the God Chief was human. The Others competed in the Settlement's games, but there was little other interaction. They were generally ignored by the Settlement's people, though the Chief believed time would eventually integrate both groups into one.

When Salt had explained the Others, Follows had been indifferent, regarding them as irrelevant to his future. But now confronted by these people, he felt endangered. He understood groups and nature; his life had been destroyed by foreign men. They had killed his father and uncle and taken his mother, cousin, aunt, and sister. He could not trust men who were not allied by community or cooperation, leaving him insecure and vicious. Could his companions not see the mortal risk, the threat to their families and future? His other difficulties within the Settlement seemed suddenly inconsequential and temporary; this problem was potentially lethal. Only killing these men guaranteed his life and safety, every alternative meant living under threat. A deep lust to eliminate these men overtook him, drowning all else.

He defiantly returned the Others' stares, challenging them, full of wrath. Unconsciously, he gripped his spear tight, his legs tensed ready to sprint, and he visualised buried weapons in the men. But his concentration was upset by his companion.

'If you're not going to help carve meat, go hunt with the other men.'

Distracted from his hateful reverie, Follows stumbled back from loathing. He struggled to recapture some equanimity, to turn his focus from murder, but he could not suppress his indignation, infuriated by his powerlessness and his companions' attitude. He needed to get away, otherwise his control might break. He turned and walked towards the other hunters, feeling ashamed by his retreat.

He immediately questioned the Chief's judgement, unable to understand how tolerating rivals was preferable to having one cohesive people. Tolerating the Others was imprudent and risked the Settlement's security. Did these people understand people? Did they think themselves somehow different from all life? He tried to remember he was ignorant compared to the Chief's divine perspective, but that could not temper his doubts. Suddenly he resented the Settlement for its weakness and ignorance.

He felt impotent, unsupported by allies, under threat from enemies, condemned to death if he acted alone. Walking away drained him and embittered him against the Settlement's attitude and the Chief. He had survived by fleeing or eliminating threats, and discarding these practices seemed both impossible and suicidal. The Settlement was suddenly unsafe and its peace obviously temporary. Each side would pursue their own interests within the same area, irrevocably leading to disputes and deepening hostilities. He knew man's combative nature; eventually peace would end.

He struggled to ignore his thoughts and feelings, trying to believe that the God Chief knew better, but instead he lapsed into indecision and fear.

Silent, hurt, and downcast, he united with the other hunters, finding them unconcerned and jovial. The men fell upon the escaping herd's trail and disappeared into the forest.

SEVENTEEN

FOLLOWS SAT UPON THE lake's banks, beneath slow clouds speckling the summer sky. At his feet, the waters lapped against the shores, their gentleness begging calm.

He watched children playing in the shallows: play-fighting and racing, arguing and gossiping, telling stories and boasting. But their play did not lighten his mood. The children's every action seemed analogous to adult behaviour, differing only in simplicity and subtlety. Childhood seemed only a preparation for adulthood, its purpose to learn enough cunning and knowledge to survive. The perspective leant the children a sinister quality, like they were rivals readying to compete against him.

The perspective was unwelcome—he had been seeking comfort. The humid day had promised many spirits by the lake, inviting him to its banks to seek their counsel. He had spoken his concerns, but no otherworldly insight had answered, leaving him as uncertain as before.

His encounter with the Others had unnerved him and shattered his peace. The more he discovered about them, the more uncomfortable he became, creating a discomfort impossible to ignore.

The Others partnered and socialised within their own

community, conducted their own gatherings and hunts. They interacted infrequently with the Settlement—as both groups were happier amongst their own people—which prohibited familiarity and friendships, increasing his foreboding and apprehension. He harboured no hate for the Others individually; it was a matter of survival, and their group threatened his future.

There had been occasional fights between the groups, sometimes fatal ones, but the Chief had always ensured peace through negotiation and by punishing those seeking revenge—always avoiding war. Peace was always the Chief's priority, no matter the tension and resentment the rivalry caused.

He suspected the Settlement did not realise its foolishness. They assumed their values were correct and would therefore be adopted by those with differing ways, that their tolerance would invite similar treatment and dissuade conflict. They did not know that attitudes and beliefs are inherited, and that if born elsewhere, they would believe differently and be convinced they were the better people.

Groups expand and confront limitations, and every concession reduces the groups autonomy, safety, power, and resources. The Settlement would gradually become more dependent on foreign mercy as the Others grew in number, limiting their ability to protect themselves and their ways. He knew the world's nature: safety was hard-fought and easily lost. As the Others expanded, so would the divide, propelling the groups towards conflict. He feared being the victim of war and knew he would feel insecure until the Others were gone.

His disquiet had pressed him to seek the spirits' advice, but they had not responded. Instead, he searched for solutions, and decided that there were two: remove the Others or forcibly integrate them into the Settlement. But he knew the Settlement was incapable of either solution, making him certain the Settlement was destined for slow erosion and conflict.

If he wanted peace, he needed to remove the Others. He had survived by escaping or eliminating threats, because whether genuinely lethal or mistakenly judged, a removed threat guaranteed safety. He had no influence, but he did not accept himself powerless to affect change. Ignoring problems worsened them, and he would not accept helplessness just because of low status.

His conviction was tempered only by his confidence in the Chief. He knew his own convictions were inferior to a god's, even a fallible one. The Chief believed time would broker a peace and merge the groups, yet Follows' experience had taught him otherwise, making his faith conflicting.

Follows felt torn by indecision and frustrated by the spirits' silence. Why did they not answer? Would Quiet's spirit ever help or forgive him? He needed his brother's guidance; he felt crippled without it. He had followed Quiet most of his life, inherited his ambition and dreams, and been balanced by his measure. He felt so alone and lost without him, especially amongst so many people.

Follows felt his own name a curse which condemned him to dependence. Even joining their old group had been Quiet's idea. He had been reluctant, but Quiet's reason had persuaded.

> 'These tracks are recent,' Follows said. 'This group is half a day away.'
>
> Prints of men, women, and children were trodden into the grass, their pattern suggesting a group of thirty. Sense argued escape, but loneliness begged congress, leaving the brothers debating. Quiet wanted to join the group but Follows thought it reckless.
>
> 'This group has a lot of dependents. They will need men,' Quiet offered.
>
> 'Every encounter with people has ended violently. We should just take two women and escape,' Follows countered.

'The men outnumber us and with women they would catch us,' returned Quiet. 'I know you don't like people, but we may never partner outside a group. We must take a chance, or we will become lonelier, grow simpler, and lose purpose.'

The words broke Follows' reservation. He knew their solitude was damaging them. Similar days and routine survival inspired little. They were losing motivation and hope. Without counterargument, he deferred to Quiet's judgement and resigned himself to risking contact.

That night the brothers killed, gutted, and butchered a fawn, readied it for cooking, then left it near the sleeping group. They retreated away, knowing their offering would invite a response. They slept well hidden and distant in case they were tracked, alternating watch to avoid surprise.

In the morning they returned, vigilant and weary of ambush. They found their fawn gone and replaced by skinned and gutted rabbits. They were either being thanked or offered peace, but either way they felt encouraged to make contact.

The brothers built a fireplace and skewered the rabbits above it. They left it unlit and waited for someone to arrive before they ate.

'What if many men arrive?' Follows asked.

'If they want peace, they won't send many. If we see many, we run,' answered Quiet.

The brothers waited, surveying in silence, nervous but hopeful. Two men did eventually arrive. Follows lit the fire and the four men ate, communicating in drawings and gestures, slowly forming a union that would bring the brothers into the group.

Follows wondered if Quiet's reasoning had partly fuelled his hunt for the Settlement, and if these memories and thoughts were being provoked by his spirit.

'Send me a sign you are here, Quiet,' he whispered over the lake.

But stillness and silence answered, saddening him. He steered his thoughts back to the present.

From the lake streaked the river which divided the Settlement and the Others. He looked at the shelters on either side, shadowed and unnatural, defying the gods' natural design. He watched Others walk to the river to bathe and drink, searching them for differences, trying to discover why they regarded themselves special. They looked and moved the same, yet he would kill them if allowed; he would not die like his father.

He felt impotent and could not steer himself from negativity. Without task to distract him, he wallowed in worry, or fantasised about confronting the Others. He dwelt within these thoughts until he was disturbed by an enormous man walking towards the lake. It was Bear, the Others' leader. Bear was the Settlement's wrestling champion and winner of every tournament for the past four seasons. His dominance had caused interest in his fights to wane, but had earned him adulation and leadership amongst the Others and the respect of the entire Settlement.

He had seen about twenty-five winters and had been named for fighting like a bear. His hair and beard were dark and plaited, his eyebrows thick, his eyes deep-set and grey. He was the tallest and heaviest man amongst both the Others and the Settlement, his size an intimidating threat of power. The crowd's excitement when Bear fought was something Follows shared. His fights were enthralling displays of strength and clinical viciousness. After his fights, Bear was reconciliatory and gracious, which Follows judged a humble act to win the crowd's admiration.

Bear wandered to the lake, tired and muddy, presumably just returned from hunting. Follows watched him undress and wade into the water to wash—heavy with muscle, shoulders abnormally wide. He imagined fighting Bear, wanting to test himself against such strength, curious how he would fare.

As Bear left the lake, the men caught each other's attention and exchanged brief stares. But Bear turned away, uninterested and keen for home. As Bear dressed, Follows' curiosity overpowered him: he wanted to see how Bear would react to being challenged. Follows called out to Bear.

'Do you think there will be war between our groups?'

Bear looked up, surprised by the question and directness. He appeared both defensive and bothered, unsure whether the question was provocative or genuine. Without knowing the appropriate reaction, Bear questioned him.

'Do you?'

'They will fight—factions cause such,' Follows replied.

His reply implicitly condemned the Others' residency, which swayed Bear towards readiness. He saw Bear stiffen, but he was undeterred from argument.

'And how would you stop this conflict?' returned Bear, his voice tinged with aggression and challenge.

'Your people should leave. You poison both sides with hostility by staying.'

Bear's eyes widened, his hands clenched, and his head lowered. Yet he did nothing. He stood, incensed by Follows, fighting against every impulse to attack.

'Your accent is foreign, you're not from the Settlement. What's your name?' Bear spat.

Bear's hostility raised Follows' own aggression, but he fought it down, knowing the situation was on the precipice of bloodily escalating.

'They call me Wild One,' he answered, his voice mixed with contempt and pretended calm.

'You don't belong here, and your distrust is groundless

aggression. Either stand behind your words and fight me, or back down like a coward.'

Bear's challenge meant wrestling—a common way young men settled animosities. Though Follows felt ashamed, he broke eye contact. He implored himself to resist being goaded, knowing he would lose. He had not sought the fight, and he would not be injured or die for pride. His silence refused the invitation. Bear left, sneering and contemptuous.

Hurt by his cravenness, Follows sank into disgrace and introversion. But inside his dejection he retraced the interaction, noticing how easily Bear had risen to provocation, a weakness perhaps. He knew he was searching for advantages should he ever fight Bear; he could not help it—he felt ashamed and wanted revenge.

Over the lake, the warped air danced in the heat, thirsty spirits slaking thirsts, deaf to his troubles. Was Quiet amongst them? Would he ever speak to him again? The sultry air trickled over his skin, asking he forget his concerns. Between his instinct and doubt he sat, frayed by their conflict.

EIGHTEEN

AS THE WARM DAYS wore away, the wind exchanged its warmth for a dying summer's cool. The leaves shed their green for the orange, red, and yellow that precede winter, coating the forest floors in colour. The weak sun shone faintly over the cooling earth, and the sky filled with crimson cloud and refracted sun. The world had calmed, and the extremes of each season were subdued and distant. The tranquil world cradled him within its peace and invited him to forget his concerns.

Follows and his companion fished in silence, each adrift in thought. His companion was called Fall—shortened from Snowfall—because of his unusual preference for winter. He was young, his hair straight and tied back, his beard short and thin. Fall was both shorter and less developed than him, but a capable and dependable fisherman.

Their boat ebbed gently, guided by the whim of the waves and wind. The sea was as serene as the season, and the wind as mellow as the sun. Follows was detached and relaxed, his thoughts roving and aimless. His eyes wandered over the sea, its surface ignited by red sunset and shadow. The gods' art was stirring, making him grateful to be alive and its witness.

Since joining the Settlement, his company with the gods and their wonders had been limited, making him sometimes forget existence beyond people. Time for thought and insight had been rare, and usually only possible when settling to sleep. But he had used his time pragmatically and devoted himself—despite his reservations—to his new life. His commitment had gifted him the language and the capability to swim, to construct boats, and to fish the sea.

He was an average fisherman, but his hunting had impressed people. The men had encouraged him to dedicate himself solely to hunting, but finally they conceded to his ambition to fish. He enjoyed both the sea's violence and tranquillity—it reflected both the majesty and mercilessness of the gods, the world, and life. Its magnificence was made more poignant by its contrasting ruthlessness, because knowing suffering was necessary to know and appreciate beauty.

The light was beginning to fade, and the shore's details were growing faint; their day's catch was small but acceptable. The other fishermen had begun paddling to shore, casting long shadows across the burnt sea. He could identify each man from their silhouette; their familiarity a reminder of their shared labours and fortunes, making him appreciate them. He wanted the Others to join them—cooperation might erase division—but he knew this wishful.

'The Others would rather war than join,' he muttered absently to himself.

He turned his attention to his companion. He was watching the sunset, distant and contemplative.

'We're done for the day,' Follows said as he brought his fishing equipment into the boat.

Fall quietly and slowly packed. Follows noticed Fall was irritated, but he said nothing, uninterested in discussion. But Fall spoke anyway.

'You attribute your nature to the Others. They aren't like you.'

Follows was stunned by the criticism and Fall's defence of the Others. He was allied and worked with Fall; how could he chastise him for criticising these potentially dangerous people? The Settlement's tolerance of the Others was incomprehensible and maddening. Even Hare, with his scepticism and directness, never condemned the Others. He had seen Hare resentful and uncomfortable when the Others were discussed, but Hare had never voiced his feelings. Such behaviour was prevalent throughout the Settlement, and without words for kindling, there could be no fire.

Unable to find fault with his behaviour, he was unsure how to respond. Silence hung over them while Follows studied Fall's expression, but it told him nothing.

'I want them gone and so should you,' Follows replied. 'They will care for their family over yours and protect each other over you,' he said coldly.

Fall faced him, riled and nervous, obviously uncomfortable and unused to confrontation.

'We have peace because we're tolerant. We had a fractious and violent past that destroyed lives and families. We must avoid past mistakes to protect people, and never sacrifice stability for bloodshed.'

'Competing peoples cause war,' Follows answered. 'People prefer their own kin and beliefs, and they will defend them. Only force can drive away threats. Pretending inaction is a solution is delusion. Defending your ways and lands safeguards your family and your people's future. Ignoring threats just delays and worsens the eventual conflict and damage. The Settlement's wars were unavoidable, but its strength won you peace. That is the past's lesson.'

Follows could not pretend further interest—their discussion was pointless and would achieve nothing. He was powerless to affect change; his words were wasted on these people. Follows fetched his oar and began paddling to shore, eager for his shelter and to escape from people. But Fall was not finished.

'You will never have your way. We are good people committed to fairness. You cannot understand our principles and decency because of your wildness.'

'Tolerance has limits, war will revisit. Time does not change man. When necessity requires it, your descendants will kill, just like your ancestors, and their opinions will echo mine,' he tersely finished.

They were the last words spoken between them. Fall leadenly fetched his oar and helped paddle them silently to shore. Fall's turned back hid his expression, but his sunken shoulders betrayed his sullen mood. The argument had soured the pleasant day and dragged Follows' thoughts back to his frustrations with the Settlement and its people. He tried to refocus on his own ambitions, the threat of the Others was beyond his control. But he knew he could never live with the Others without fear.

They rowed in silence until the boat glided onto the sand. They were the last boat to dock, and only Salt remained. They hauled the boat clear of the waves, emptied it, and turned it over. Salt walked to greet them but remained quiet, noticing the tension.

When everything was put away, Fall departed, without farewell, with his share of the catch. Follows stood, barefoot in the sand, watching Fall walk up the beach and disappear into the darkness, wearily accepting that staying in the Settlement was becoming untenable.

He felt surrounded by fools and exasperated by their poor judgement. Their attitudes were draining and their perspectives childish, and neither argument nor reason could reach them. He needed to be free of people and recapture the peace and clarity that company prohibited. He needed unplanned and spontaneous days and an unpredictable future again. Predictability stole wonder and excitement and damaged vitality. Schedules and structure bored and fatigued him. The Settlement's benefits were not worth its costs anymore, he needed the wild and its uncertainty. As he was convincing himself to leave the Settlement, Salt interrupted him.

'Clear night,' came Salt's voice.

Follows had not the energy to reply; he remained still, staring after Fall's vanished figure, dispirited and drained. He acknowledged the old man with a nod, but was too distracted to offer more.

'Come and keep me and the stars company before you retire for the night,' asked Salt.

Follows turned to the old man. He was sitting on the deserted beach, wearing the amiable smile worn into his face by a lifetime of use. Despite his need to leave the Settlement, Salt's warmth was difficult to reject.

'I wouldn't be good conversation tonight, Salt,' he said gently.

'Perfect, because I have a story, and I don't want to be interrupted,' Salt returned.

Follows sighed, too weary and downcast to argue. He crossed to Salt and sat beside the old man. He reclined against a rock and stared over the sea. The pregnant Moon had risen through the aether to lighten the night. She streaked trails of blue moonshine across the sea, creating ethereal paths into the gods' immaterial lands. Whatever his situation, the gods never tired of painting for their children. Comforted by this thought, he felt more patient, better able to endure a story. Salt interrupted the waves as he began.

'Many seasons ago, I was caught in a terrible storm, alone at sea. Unable to fight the conditions, I gave away control and let the tempest guide me. I fought through the night to remain with my boat, oar held tightly to prevent its loss, clinging desperately as the waves attacked and overturned me. But I defied the sea's efforts to drown me. Gradually, its anger and maliciousness abated, the storm clouds parted, and a beautiful morning chased away the dark. As the shadows lifted, I saw a distant mountain interrupting the horizon, but it was not our world, Wild One. The gods had taken me to a land hidden inside the infinite sea. I was overwhelmed and emotional, my worldview broken. I wondered what impossible creatures lived within these lands and what strange creations the gods might have built there. I was cast into indecision, unable to decide whether to explore this new world or begin for home. I dithered uncertainly, until finally clarity made my decision easy. This new world could give me nothing I wanted. My family, friends, and community were at home. My imagination had overflowed with fantastical possibilities, and curiosity had almost swayed me, but sense reached me. I would not risk everything I loved, and had built, for imaginings. I had fantasised a better life without even seeing the shore, as if life's challenges would cease to exist in a new place. We all believe our difficulties can be attributed to the place we live, the work we do, and the people around us, and that somehow a new life will liberate us. But our problems are universal and sewn into life. No amount of new beginnings will spare you the hardship of building a good life. Expectation and ambitions are great and necessary, but don't let them ruin your chance at building happiness.'

The men stared silently out to sea, Follows adrift in conflicting thoughts and Salt in memory. Salt climbed to his feet with an exaggerated groan, still wearing his wrinkled smile. He rapped Follows on the back, and began up the beach towards the Settlement, taking some fish with him.

As Salt approached the shadows, Follows called after him.

'Do you still wonder what the new world was like, Salt?'

Salt looked around at him and nonchalantly shrugged.

'I wonder about it almost every day, Wild One.'

The old man turned and walked into the dark, leaving Follows alone on the empty beach, unsure how to feel.

NINETEEN

FOLLOWS WANDERED BACK FROM the beach, passed through the Settlement, and fled into the wilderness. He knew not whether he was leaving indefinitely or temporarily—his escape was reflexive. Frustration propelled him, solitude and freedom from people encouraged him.

He walked to the Settlement's bordering hill, but once descending, he fell into a lope, then a sprint. He had no plan or destination, just an impulse seeking release. He ran across the dark grasslands, through woodland, over streams and valleys, under moonlight and stars. His breath rose like smoke and sweat trickled his face. The night seemed a dark ocean, and he its lone traveller.

The further he ran, the more stress fell away, and the greater his exertion, the freer he felt. He felt his shoulders relax and his irritation fade, slowly lessening his exasperation. People's suffocating systems and attitudes fell behind and became unimportant. The Settlement's inaction and weakness began infuriating him less, and his lack of influence grew less disappointing. He pushed on until his chest heaved and his legs strained, but neither could temper his ferocity.

He ran until a rocky cliff interrupted the land, its dark heights inexplicably inviting. Without pause, he leapt upon its mossy crags and drove up its face. His ascent was unthinking and aggressive, his hands and feet furious. He thrust himself towards the heavens, escaping the grasslands below.

He burst onto the summit and tore forwards until he was eventually arrested by a precipice. The severed ground plummeted into shadow, its edge overlooking huge sprawling lowlands. The pregnant Moon and her children rained starlight onto the ashen world, dyeing it in blues and whites. Beneath his mountain, moonshine reflecting streams spilled from a lake, igniting the dark grasslands with glittering trails. The lake perfectly mirrored the night sky, undisturbed by wind or ripple, doubling the Moon and her stars.

Follows sank to his knees, breathing heavy, arms sagging. He looked over the nocturnal land and realised he had never been here. He slumped to sitting, his breathing already slowing, his composure returning. He felt the world's tranquillity permeate him, and his aggression and stress fell away.

His felt reminded of his flight when Mane died—overwhelmed and driven away. Her memory revived an irreparable ache, but he gladly suffered it to relive their time together. He became nostalgic and wistful, and knew their time together to be his happiest. But he reminisced without resistance, revisiting memories with fondness and bereavement.

Thinking of Mane was saddening but calming, giving him opportunity to reacquire perspective. He thought about Salt's story and understood its meaning: time, work, and patience built a better life, and running from difficulties helped nothing. His internal conflict had evidently been transparent to Salt. He supposed some feelings were shared burdens, identifiable to those similarly afflicted.

Salt was right, but even time and work guaranteed nothing. Many other things also influenced success: the calibre of competition, the opinions of others, the status of allies and family, and the frequency and magnitude of opportunities. Maybe the same difficulties did exist everywhere, but he believed a better life was always possible. Without that hope, life felt confined.

When Salt decided against exploring the new world, he gave up hope of a better life, and committed his remaining days to the Settlement and its people. Follows doubted he could confine himself so consciously. He was bored by the familiar, was invigorated by novelty, and dreamed ceaselessly of possibilities. Maybe ambition could destroy happiness, but he also knew that abandoning dreams damaged the spirit. This made him wonder if he was capable of the fulfilment other people enjoyed. He would have sailed for the new world without hesitation. He could not live haunted by curiosity. Maybe new beginnings did not end old problems, but he would never be cowed by fear.

Follows knew his fear of the Others was coercing him to return to the wilderness, even though loneliness and aimlessness awaited him there. The Settlement could give him family, friendships, and the respect necessary for pride. He needed to overcome his problems and achieve these goals, otherwise he would become lonelier, grow simpler, and lose purpose.

Gentle winds trickled over him and chased away exertion's heat. His closest friend had arrived to share his solitude and thoughts. He felt relaxed and his mind felt clear. He reclined against a rock and let his body slacken. His gaze fell upwards into the stars and travelled across the night. No cloud blighted the sky. The Moon burnt against the abyssal sky and showered the world in light. Below him the grasslands danced in the wind, countless stems soughing in harmony, rippling like waves upon the sea.

The world was the gods' divine expression, the nocturnal exhibition a reflection of their feelings. They wrote their passions with physical creations and built the living with hints of their consciousness. Their passionate craft evoked feelings he could never convey, and his every attempt only undermined their profound impact.

Perhaps only the gods' language could communicate the feelings their artistry inspired.

He was proud he understood the gods better than the Settlement's people. He had listened to the Settlement's stories of their gods and been disconcerted by their consistent theme. All their gods had human form but possessed supernatural abilities, such as immense strength and speed, immortality, magic, or flight.

But the gods were not human and did not think or behave like humans. They had their own motivations and feelings, their own trials and concerns. He knew this to be true because man could not create the world's complexity, or move its enormity, or sculpt life. Only gods in their unimaginable forms could design, build, and manage the universe. Could the Sun God look upon himself with mortal eyes; or lift himself with earthly hands? The Settlement's people were so immersed in human company that they believed man an exceptional creature, that the gods shared their desires and behaviours.

But their stories had helped him understand the Settlement's people. Excepting the God Chief, all the Settlement's gods were fictions invented to reflect the freedoms people wished for themselves. These superhumans were freed from man's labour, hierarchy, servility, and structured lives. They were not bound by social convention, physical limits, age, competition, and survival. He realised the people were unconsciously uncomfortable with their lives and needed escape through fantasies of freedom and importance. All their order and safety did not make them happy.

Knowing the Settlement's gods were fictions freed Follows from fearing them. He could connive and manipulate to advance himself in the Settlement without their gods intervening. He wanted to believe that the Chief was also mortal, but the rich lands and outlandish Settlement disallowed such beliefs. Fortunately, the Chief and his ancestors had foolishly restricted their abilities by assuming human forms.

Knowing that only he was responsible for acquiring his desired life, and that little opposition existed in the Settlement, Follows decided to plot and seize what he wanted. Salt was right, escaping the Settlement guaranteed nothing, but his cunning could elevate him. What was the alternative? To live in fear, to harbour hate, to bear children vulnerable to attack. When young, he had run from men, but he was no longer a child. He would not waste time climbing hierarchies fairly, he would forcibly realise his ambitions, achieve influence, and confront the Others. The only obstacle was the God Chief, whom he would avoid challenging.

Follows lay against the stone and built plans through the night. He grew excited for the future and confident of achieving power. He was shivering under the wind, but he was oblivious; his mind was consumed by ideas and anticipation, lifting him from worldly concerns.

As he planned, he thought of something about the Chief that could prove useful—his breathing. It betrayed a human vulnerability—he could potentially be drowned or choked. It might be possible to kill the Chief, and if conflict became unavoidable, he would find a way to starve him of air.

He suspected the Wind God was guiding his mind. Their thoughts had become inextricable and symbiotic, his divine suggestion indistinguishable from his own realisations. He knew the gods flowed through the living and pushed their creations towards betterment. The gods were more vocal when man was alone, just as being surrounded made them communicate with man less, making him wonder how much guidance he had recently missed. He could feel the Wind God encouraging him and promising support, and though he had neglected their friendship recently, their bond transcended offence. He would let the Wind God guide him; Follows' trust was absolute.

As the stars travelled the night sky, his schemes slowly shaped into a final design to capture authority, gain leadership, and evict the Others. The means had been there: Bear's temper, the Chief's tolerance, and wrestling to resolve discord.

Follows excitedly considered his plan, nervous but enthusiastic. He remained until drowsiness intruded and made his thoughts dreamlike, then he climbed into the starlight and began his return towards the Settlement. His steps felt lighter and his body looser—his stresses discarded, his mind ordered.

But as he grew closer to the Settlement, he found himself suddenly fixated on Salt's new world. He noticed his fascination and knew his curiosity would only deepen. He just hoped that the unknowing would not become obsession.

TWENTY

THE WARM SUMMER DAYS gradually wilted, and winter invaded. The Winter God blanketed the earth in white, turned the lakes into ice, and stripped the forests. Men and women navigated the world wrapped in thicker furs, careful of the cruel winds and lethal colds.

The earth's produce died, and the hunt compensated. Men ventured out further, fur clad and prayer blessed, hunting to sustain the Settlement. Inside the shelters, fires burnt ceaselessly, protecting their makers and children. The winds whisked away the fire smoke and buried it in the mists and fogs. Animals retreated to sleep, and birdsong disappeared.

The winter had raised Follows to prominence. His hunting talents and resilience had earned him notice, respect, and leadership over many hunts. Like the great predators, independence had made him strong. An arduous life had grown his competence, and his struggles had given him resolve. His peers were different—their easier lives had made them less driven. Follows had worked fanatically until he was one of the Settlement's best providers, affording him a reputation as a trusted, fearless, and dedicated individual—a regard he planned to exploit before nightfall.

Follows was heading a party of five men. They lay in the snow, waiting, breath buried in their furs, hiding behind a hill. Follows peered over the hill's brow, watching the deer push through the snow-laden winds towards the forest, waiting for their other hunters to charge the deer.

From the forest burst six men with spears raised, shouting over the loud winds, wading towards the deer through deep snows. The men had no chance of approaching within a spear throw—the deer vaulted away before spears were within reach. The herd raced towards Follows, climbing his hill, leaving their assailants distant, entering his ambush.

As the deer summited the hill, his men attacked. Their six spears leapt through the air and brought down a doe. The remaining herd hurtled frantically onward, disappearing into the mist. The men immediately set upon their kill and carved her into transportable loads. Some would return food to the Settlement; the rest would make for a hunting outpost to eat and warm themselves.

Follows would return to the Settlement. He had foregone returning three times to continue heading the hunt, waiting for the right opportunity. He and two other men would return the meat to the Settlement—men he planned to kill.

The hunters finished cutting and distributing the meat, loaded themselves, bid farewell, and separated. He and the two men began homeward while his hunters headed for the nearest shelter. The men accompanying him were Others, their participation in this hunt his doing.

Follows had deliberately steered his men towards a herd being hunted by Others, knowing their groups would argue over the deer. He had pursued this outcome all winter, but unpredictable herds, and ensuring hunts were successful, had complicated its arrangement. But finally, the groups had clashed, and he had brokered the peace by insisting they cooperate. Follows had the Others frighten the herd into his men's ambush, agreeing that afterwards they would split the meat and separate.

Now alone with the two Others, he prepared himself, knowing he might never again get such an opportunity. He knew his elevated status was temporary and dependent on his usefulness during the winter. When the snows melted and hunting grew easy, his value and authority would lessen, making it harder to manipulate situations and execute plans.

The cliff he had plotted upon had reminded him of a brutal conflict he and Quiet had fought. The memory had inspired his plan: the Others would be killed; Bear would suspect and challenge him, but the Settlement would believe him innocent and defend him. Tension and suspicion on both sides would make cohabitation impossible. There would be war, or the Others would be driven away. Either outcome would culminate in a more lasting and stable peace, and he would emerge a hero. He would raise his status, attract women's notice, and gain authority, finally giving him the life he wanted.

The memory of the encounter he and Quiet had fought, that had inspired his plan, stirred him to fervency. It had been eight summers ago, when not yet fully grown. Quiet's cunning had saved them, and now his example would guide Follows to the life he wanted.

> *The brothers retreated through the summer woodland. They had been chased three days and two nights without pause, leaving them near exhaustion. Neither had managed more than a sleepwalk before a stumble interrupted that little rest.*
>
> *Three days before, they had unknowingly wandered into some group's territory and encountered people. An immediate chase had ensued from which they had barely escaped. Initially, they believed the*

men were only frightening them away to protect their families, but after a day and night, they knew it was more serious. The relentless pace felt fuelled by hatred and revenge, leading the brothers to assume they had been mistaken for enemies.

Follows was on the verge of collapse, but Quiet forced him onwards. His fear had initially masked his pain, but now hunger and exhaustion made painful each moment. His legs were failing, slowing him, making him realise he would be caught. He was drained to staggering, his body incapable of matching his will. Yet Quiet's coercion kept hauling him back from collapse and reinvigorating his nerve.

They took unusual and disordered routes through the thick forest, hoping to confuse and evade their pursuers. But the men expertly trailed them without much delay, never stopping to rest or eat. Quiet led their retreat through the humid maze of trees and underbrush, trying to find a waterfall they had visited nine days previously.

The brothers finally emerged into the clearing that surrounded the waterfall, its height about fifteen men. Water cascaded down the jagged cliffs into shallow pools which streamed into the forest. On each side of the falls were rockfaces, easily climbable and dry. They stopped beside the stream and Quiet hurriedly instructed Follows.

'We'll both walk into the stream; you exit downriver and hide. Keep sight of the waterfall and avoid leaving footprints. I'll exit the stream on the far bank and score two trails to the rockface. I'll climb to the summit and move large stones near the edge. When the men arrive, they'll follow my tracks and climb

after me. As they're ascending, I'll crush them with the rocks. When you see me attack, run out and spear the climbing men. Together we will kill them all.'

Follows looked into his brother's red-stained eyes. His skin was dirty and pale, sweat soaked and wretched, but his stare was fanatic and merciless. It roused Follows and convinced him survival was possible. No further discussion was necessary, and the brothers separated to their tasks.

He followed the currents and exited downstream, careful to leave no tracks. He buried himself inside thick brambles on the forest's edge and peered at the cliff through leaves and thorns. He held a spear in each hand, anger simmering in each poised limb. He expected to wait awhile, but the men quickly arrived—the brothers had misjudged the men's proximity; they had been on the verge of capture.

Five men burst from the forest. They barely slowed before they saw Quiet's trail and bounded through the stream towards it. They followed the wet footprints to the rockface and threw themselves at the climb, disregarding strategy or caution.

He watched the men progress up the cliff and near its top. He feared Quiet was unaware of how close the men were and would miss his chance, almost causing him to scream a warning. But before he could, his brother appeared on the precipice, carrying an enormous rock.

Quiet stumbled to the nearest man and drove the rock down upon him. The man noticed his brother just before the rock connected, but he was powerless to respond. The rock smashed the man from the cliff *and crushed him into the rocky ground, shattering his body.*

Within a breath, Follows had sprinted from cover, ripping his skin on thorns and branches. The men began screaming at his brother, climbing faster, apoplectic, desperate for revenge. Before Follows reached the cliff, Quiet had retrieved another rock and positioned himself above another man. He hurled the rock down upon the man, who could only reflexively raise his arm. The rock tore the man from the cliff, and he plummeted onto the rock floor.

Follows ran behind another man and flung his spear into him. The man involuntarily stiffened, his grip loosened, and he plunged onto the rock beneath, twisting, broken, and dying. Another man realised how vulnerable he was on the rockface and leapt ten men's heights onto the ground. He fell hard and buckled to his knees. Follows quickly pivoted and launched his second spear into the kneeling man's ribs. The man fell back, choking, coughing blood, his death throes violent and contorted.

The final man reached the cliff's peak, but only momentarily. As he pulled himself over the verge, Quiet's kick connected with his jaw. The man fell unconscious onto the ground below and ruptured his head.

While Quiet descended the rockface, Follows recovered a spear, and moved amongst the wounded, impaling and twisting to quicken the men's deaths, and ensure their threat was extinguished.

The brothers embraced, shaken, exhausted, and elated. Conflict's fervour shook their bodies and intoxicated their minds, making expression and composure difficult, but neither brother needed to communicate their relief and exhilaration. They had been outnumbered but survived, and bettered older men. They finally felt like adults, empowered and ascended, able to discard the insecurity of being fatherless, proved they were not defenceless. They understood each other's elation, and it bound them even closer.

The incident had been Quiet's legacy—resilience and courage despite adversity. Follows did not know if he was Quiet's equal, but he had always strived to imitate his example. He would not betray his memory by compromising. He would relentlessly pursue the ambitions they had always shared until they were achieved.

Ice laden winds struck the three men as they laboured knee deep through the snow towards the Settlement. Snow and fog churned together to hide the distance, but the men knew the territory and needed only a familiar tree to navigate from. Surrounding the Settlement were ravines and cliffs, at which Follows had placed boulders. Whichever way the men returned, he would have an opportunity to kill the Others and make it appear an accident.

They trudged until a rocky cliff emerged from concealment. Its sight, and their desperation to escape the wind, quickened their advance. Follows made sure to arrive first, and immediately began climbing, conscious that he must summit before the other men. His fingers were numb and his grip weak, but he struggled upwards, fuelled by purpose. The Others climbed more slowly and cautiously, giving Follows the time he needed.

Follows summited and was immediately reunited with the wind's harshness. He grimaced as the cold assaulted him, every muscle stiffening and tense. He searched, eyes narrowed by snow and wind, for the rock he had placed atop the cliff. He saw it, submerged beneath snow, almost hidden. Follows descended upon it and began levering it towards the cliff's edge. His legs forced down through the snow onto the hidden ground beneath. Under the weight, his back warped and legs burned, but he barely noticed; he was wild, belligerent, and fanaticised.

Finally, the boulder shifted. He hauled it to the cliff's edge, cast a cursory glance at the two ascending men to ensure they were in position, and then drove the deadly instrument forwards. Neither man noticed the boulder falling towards them. They were absorbed in their climb, and died never knowing of the attack—struck from the cliff and crushed.

Follows stared downwards through the snowstorm at the remains of what once were men. The wind beat against his back, and snow whipped across his face, but neither distracted him from the scene. The men were ripped apart, their blood lashed across the ground, momentarily staining the uniform whiteness. Already, the Winter God began washing away the blood with fresh snowfall and burying the men.

Follows' long exhale expressed his mixed feelings of achievement and regret. The carnage momentarily damaged his resolve, but he was too committed to falter long. He needed war, or the threat of war, to achieve peace, and now war was close. The Settlement was peaceful, but even the peaceful put aside peace when threatened. He would bring that threat to them.

Follows began slowly traipsing towards the Settlement, underneath the escalating snowstorm and darkening skies. He hunkered into the bitter winds, possessed by ambition, feeling in control of his destiny.

TWENTY-ONE

FOLLOWS STARED OVER THE fire at the thoughtful and disturbed man. They sat alone, skins tinged by flame, faces serious. Their shadows flickered upon the hide walls, and warmth swirled around them, bodies comfortable despite the uncomfortable company. The two men sat silently, interrupted only by the tempest outside and the shelter's rippling walls.

After killing the two men, Follows had walked into the Others' camp to inform Bear. Bear had sent away his women and children for their privacy, then sat by the fire as Follows gave his account.

Follows told Bear how the boulder had dislodged during the climb, fortunately missing him, but killing Bear's men. Bear had remained impassive throughout, his stare level and unfeeling, cold and scrutinising. He was an imposing and intimidating man. Follows knew that Bear personified the Others' belief in their underlying superiority. They felt protected under Bear, making them more tribal. He believed that only inferior numbers dissuaded the Others from seeking greater power, and he doubted that reluctance would last.

Follows sat in the uncomfortable silence waiting to be accused. He knew Bear doubted his story, their previous meeting had ensured it. Bear was expressionless but Follows felt his suspicion. He could tell Bear was desperate to confront him—as he had anticipated. Bear's predictability made him manipulatable, and consequently a reliable instrument.

The silence dragged and strained until finally Bear threw away his reserve. Bear knew Follows' opinion of the Others, and now two had died in his company; it was too coincidental.

'Rocks don't throw themselves from cliffs,' Bear said coldly, laying bare his accusation.

The tension heightened, Follows' chest beat faster, his limbs felt light, but he retained composure and acted shocked instead. They would fight, and he wanted some doubt to temper Bear's ferocity and make him exercise some restraint when they clashed. Follows feigned insult and rose to his feet. He stared down at the large man and issued his rehearsed challenge.

'Your accusation is unacceptable, and your distrust is groundless aggression. Either stand behind your words and fight me, or back down like a coward.'

Bear visibly reddened, his teeth gritted, and his breath deepened. Hearing his own words provoked an anger that disallowed him speech, but Follows took this as acceptance.

'Noon tomorrow at the wrestling grounds. Inform the Others, I'll inform the Settlement.'

The men held eyes, neither flinching nor speaking, gripped by animosity. Follows turned, walked to the entrance, and exited into the night, rattled by nervousness and excitement. The snowstorm greeted and attacked him, but he barely noticed, he was too consumed in plans.

He crossed the frozen river, bound for the combat grounds and Hare's shelter. He would inform Hare of the accident, Bear's accusation, and tomorrow's fight, confident the news would propagate to everyone before noon. The Settlement would think him brave, righteous, and foolish for wanting to punish Bear's accusation and defend his honour. The Others would react with anger and suspicion: their men had died in Follows' company, and now he challenged their leader.

Then he would kill Bear, further dividing the two groups. The Others would believe all the deaths deliberate and want revenge, the Settlement would believe the deaths accidental, and defend him. Living together would become tense and ugly; war would become likely. The groups would have to separate, or they would fight. Either way, he would extinguish the Others' threat.

He would triumph over Bear and earn influence, respect, and status. He would be the epicentre of the conflict and positioned to lead. The life he wished for felt within his grasp. The Settlement could give him everything he wanted, but until the Others were gone, he would never feel at peace.

Although he would kill Bear, he did not dislike him. He admired Bear's candour and strength, but he was an obstacle to evicting the Others. He knew Bear was a superior fighter, but he was unworried about defeat. When watching Bear fight, he had noticed an exploitable pattern. It was not enough to win, but combined with another plan, it was lethal.

Follows approached and entered the combat grounds. He dug through the snow and into the mud, then buried a jagged stone, half protruding from the ground. He covered the stone with snow and smoothed the surface. Tonight's snowfall would disguise his visit, so tomorrow nobody would suspect there had been any interference. When finished, he made for Hare's shelter.

By nightfall tomorrow, his regard would be changed, people would be divided, he would have the Settlement's support, and he would use his position to meet and steer the Chief. The life he and Quiet had dreamed of was close, and the Settlement's future safety would be secured. The bloodshed was a necessary cost.

TWENTY-TWO

FOLLOWS WOKE EARLY THE next morning. Last night's fireplace smouldered beside him, emitting wisps of smoke devoid of heat. Outside, the wind whipped across his shelter, whistling and assaulting, aggressive and stirring, urging him to rise. He was reluctant to leave his bedding's warmth, but the imminent contest quickly focused his mind.

Finally, he discarded his thoughts and forced himself up into the cold. He dressed and ventured outside, hoping fresh air would ease his nerves. He stepped into weak sunlight and found yesterday's storm gone. Faint light sporadically pierced the overcast sky; the snowfall had ceased, and birdsong had returned. It was the clearest weather in twenty days. The Winter God had mellowed for his fight, and given him conditions that would encourage attendance, making him grateful.

He breathed deeply, filling his chest with cold. He saw people casting him serious and curious glances, or waving and wishing him well. It seemed everyone had heard of his fight. There was no condemnation, just goodwill and prayers. People were sympathetic, not angry, their thoughts displayed in their expressions: he was brave but foolish, too proud and headstrong; he would lose.

When people approached and wished him well, he thanked them, feeling simultaneously empowered and embarrassed by the encouragement; praise since childhood had been rare. He walked to Hare's shelter, acknowledging blessings from passers-by, feeling uplifted by people's support and respect. He had thought many would be critical, but they just saw a freak tragedy, Bear's emotional allegation, and Follows' prideful response—nobody saw his dispute causing any significant consequences.

After visiting the combat grounds the previous night, Follows had informed Hare of the accident, Bear's accusation, and the fight. Hare had listened, and expressed some concern, but not much, he had seen tensions ignite and fade many times before. Despite Hare's disinterest, he had invited Follows to return in the morning to eat with him. Behind the paternal gesture, Follows saw both Hare's disapproval and his understanding of young men's impulsiveness. Hare withheld his criticism—it served no purpose. Instead, he offered kindness to someone isolated and facing danger without family or close friends. Follows had gratefully accepted, seeing an opportunity to befriend someone influential and increase his chances of solidifying power when Bear was dead.

Follows knew Hare thought his conflict ridiculous and inconsequential. Hare was accustomed to brokering resolutions after hostilities, but Follows would ensure escalation. The Others suspected him already, and when he killed Bear, they would be convinced of his insidiousness. Then only revenge would appease them. The Settlement would believe him innocent and defend him, leading inexorably to deepening divisions, separation, or war.

The Settlement and the Others would watch Bear die. Afterwards, shock, accusations, defence, and arguments would follow. As tensions increased, he would be positioned to speak, and empowered to resolve the discord. He would implore both sides to separate to keep their futures peaceful, and most would recognise this sensible; the alternative was far worse.

Once his plan was backed by most, the God Chief would have to separate the groups. If the Others violently resisted, the Settlement would retaliate, overwhelm, and defeat them. Whether peacefully or forcefully, the Others and their threat would be evicted, as would his fears. He would emerge influential, his position would attract a partner, and he would know his children's futures safe.

These thoughts had been travelled over many times, but his nerves disallowed him peace. He arrived at Hare's home, tired of his own mind, and found the entrance drawn and the insides flame-lit. Follows requested admission, and Hare replied with his usual impatience.

'Come in and stop making me shout.'

Follows stooped into the flushed shelter and found Hare cooking. He sat himself on furs near the fire and waited. His apprehension was straining and begged distraction. Needing to assess whether Hare would assist him when Bear was dead, Follows attempted conversation.

'After the fight, we must convince the Chief to end the divisions which caused it,' he told Hare.

Hare did not look up and ventured no reply, but he nodded absently, his face inexpressive and opinion unreadable. Deterred from attempting further conversation, Follows left Hare to consider his words.

The two men waited for the meat to cook, then Hare passed him some food. Follows thanked him and tried to eat despite his nerves. Hare sat beside him facing the fire. Follows' stomach was reluctant, but his fear of being weakened by hunger forced his efforts. They ate in silence until Hare interrupted.

'You think very practically for someone facing danger, Wild One,' Hare said.

Follows was immediately concerned that Hare suspected him of deviousness. He inspected the old man but found him impenetrable. If Hare thought him groundlessly confident, he might suspect he would cheat; or that he had orchestrated the entire situation by deliberately killing the two Others. But Follows steadied himself. He realised that any suspicions were without evidence and unprovable. Hare did not know his motivations, Follows just needed to guide him away from any suspicion.

'I won't let Bear's accusation go unpunished,' Follows began. 'But it's these divisions which caused this fight. Division causes suspicion, suspicion causes resentment, resentment causes hostility, and hostility causes conflict. I want unity and your help. We must safeguard the Settlement's peace and future.'

His words were sincere, and he hoped they would argue his innocence. But Hare looked unmoved, his glance condescending.

'Go have your fight, Wild One, and then get on with your life. Now finish eating and get some rest.'

Hare's words were indifferent and promised nothing, but at least he seemed unconcerned about underhandedness.

They ate in silence, gazes attached to flame, each elsewhere. Follows finished his food and lay to rest. He reclined into bison hides, coveting the darkness behind closed eyes. The world disappeared and thought repossessed him, but he was content to think away the time until noon. He noticed his breathing was fast, and concentrated on slowing it, striving to relax.

Inside the darkness he fought Bear. He rehearsed each conceivable scenario and every reaction and attack. He recalled Bear's fights and watched him closely, analysing his movements and timing, looking for weaknesses. He had done this many times, but he believed it readied him. Despite intending to cheat, he still needed to manoeuvre Bear into position, which was the most dangerous part of his plan.

He rehearsed until it grew repetitive and provoked impatience, making him eager to fight. To any observer, he appeared relaxed and unconcerned about the contest, but inside he was violent and restless. He drifted through the dark, grasping for composure, until finally interrupted. Hare prodded him and instantly awakened his readiness and viciousness. Hare looked at him, still inscrutable.

'Let's get this foolishness over with, Wild One.'

Follows stared up at Hare and found him neither accusing nor condemning. They held eyes momentarily before Follows nodded.

Follows rose; his focus sharpened, his breathing deepened, and aggression numbed his limbs. His periphery fogged and his surroundings faded. Hare disappeared and all existence became the fight. He stepped outside and walked towards the combat grounds, crushing snow underfoot, Hare unnoticed beside him. He walked through the deserted Settlement, a dark creature wearing savagery. His back shivered, thought drowned, his shoulders tensed.

When he approached the combat ground, he barely noticed the sea of people. Countless conversations filled the air with an unintelligible murmur, but his arrival quieted it. Hundreds of curious eyes watched him, bodies clustered together, expressions curious. He felt the tension and anticipation, each spectator captivated. The audience parted and carved him a path to the combat ground. He stepped through the crowd, his concentration completely focused, until applause shattered the silence.

The Settlement was cheering his courage, praying for him. His brutal trance broke. He looked around at the people united behind him, subdued by their support. He was their representative, and their cheers were the embodiment of their resentment for the Others. His side had already acquitted him of wrongdoing and heralded him a hero for challenging defamation. They believed he walked knowingly into certain defeat, and it earned him adulation.

He saw something else. To these people, he personified the average individual confronting his superiors and defying his inferior position. He reflected the bravery each of these average people admired and could possess themselves if pushed. He was the evidence that the ordinary were also capable of courageousness and defiance.

But he knew he was unlike these people. They had not endured his horrors, hardship, violence, and traumas. He was his past, grown without the Settlement's security and support. He had been forced resilient, stubborn, and stoic. They did not see his scars; their cause and his past life were extraneous and unrelatable. They saw an average man facing their invincible champion—but they would see a different man afterwards.

He ignored the applause and refocused his bloody concentration. He looked across the battleground and saw Bear. They locked eyes, and both their expressions grew cruel. Bear was full of contempt for him and the crowd, but untroubled by Follows' support. His arms were folded across his enormous bare chest, indifferent to the winter wind assaulting him. His body proclaimed his inhuman strength, and his disdain displayed his eagerness to use it.

Their malevolent stares killed the crowd's cheers. A dreadful silence intruded. He and Bear searched each other and grew radicalised by the other's severity. Without disengaging eyes, Follows undressed above the waist and cast his furs outside the grounds. A few overwrought moments passed before Bear spoke.

'Let's forgo any speeches and end this.'

Bear strode towards him. Follows stayed still, watching the giant ferociously close, seeing his maliciousness, waiting until he was in position. Then Follows unleashed himself and sprinted wildly towards Bear. The men crashed into each other, possessed of enmity, savagely embracing. Cheers and roars erupted again and rained upon the oblivious fighters.

Follows was immediately overpowered and wrenched off-balance, but he slipped downwards and seized Bear's legs. He violently twisted them and tackled Bear into the snow, then dived upon him, hands stabbing out to strangle. But Bear never allowed him near. He pulled Follows to his chest, wrapped his arms around his neck, and crushed him. Follows was trapped, unable to breathe, ending his chance of fair victory.

To every observer, Follows' inevitable defeat had arrived. But

Follows had anticipated this predicament. He had seen Bear asphyxiate opponents this way many times, but experience had taught him how to escape. Though his arms and body were bound, his legs were free. He pulled them inwards until in a squatting position, then he began lifting Bear. His legs and back strained and shook, his senses began darkening, and his body convulsed for air, but he continued heaving until standing. The world had turned dark and reality distant, but he held onto consciousness long enough to pivot, labour a few steps, and ruthlessly crash them both into the ground.

Bear's head snapped back and struck the rock he had hidden in the snow. A dull crack accompanied the spray of blood rupturing from Bear's head. His arms released Follows and fell limply into the blood-spattered snow.

Follows surfaced from near unconsciousness, gasping for air. He collapsed beside his dead opponent, watching blood pour from Bear, colouring the winter ground. Bear spasmed, his eyelids flickered, and his blind eyes rolled upwards. Blood pooled around his head, soaking and spreading into the snow. The audience went silent. The champion lay dead, his death sudden, unexpected, and gruesome. Everyone watched, transfixed and horrified, disbelieving and stunned. The atmosphere disallowed Follows celebration, but relief was easy.

On weak legs Follows slowly stood. Cold air caressed his pulverised body, and his breath streamed into the winds. He looked over the stupefied audience and watched the violent reality permeate them. They were gentle people, softened by comfortable lives, unused to such bloodshed. They avoided the violence he readily employed, even when peace might damage their long-term stability. Their ancestors had bought their peaceful lives with war, and now their descendants' peacefulness was inviting war into their lives.

Shouts ended the quiet, erupting from a group coalesced together. There were many different claims, but all amounted to the same thing: accusations of deviousness and malice. It was the Others, and as intended, they suspected him.

Then more shouts defending him quickly followed, turning the atmosphere ugly. Men screamed at each other, accusing and chastising, challenging and threatening. Some called for calm, others for apologies. He let the tension heighten until everyone was affected and fights were close, then he called over the shouting and everyone turned to him. He was the centre of the conflict, his right to speak earned. He had captured regard and exploded his influence, and now he needed only to direct the audience. With pretended upset, he spoke.

'The Settlement's divisions caused this accident. One group can expand freely, two groups expand into each other. By just following your own ways and providing for your families, you will deprive others, embittering those people. This bitterness will only grow and make conflicts more frequent. Ignoring problems solves nothing, pretending they don't exist grows them. Both our groups must stop risking our futures. We must separate peacefully and stop living in tension and suspicion.'

He paused to let the crowd appreciate his words. Nobody spoke or challenged, some nodded agreement, most looked uncertain. In some faces he found support, others nothing. He saw the Others both angry and devastated. Some poured loathing onto him, some, agreement. They knew their residency contentious, and most hated living with the resentment.

'With your support, I will visit the Chief and discuss separating. And when this ugliness is over, we will all be free from tribalism and our futures more peaceful. We will build cohesive communities without division, safe for our children to inherit, free to grow without restriction.'

His words reached people and persuaded the unsure, uniting the majority in agreement. Murmurs of support quickly turned into endorsing shouts, and those disagreeing were drowned.

Follows had won, he had the backing to force change from the Chief.

He had emerged from the fight transcended in stature and entitled to lead. He would remake the Settlement, guide, and unite it behind him. He was close to the life he wanted and was indifferent to the method. Bear had lived honourably and died ignominiously; his honesty and strength had earned him no mercy from injustice. But Follows was alive and elevated, celebrating his triumph and prospects, in control of his future and liberated from powerlessness.

This was the world's way: right and wrong mattered less than who won. The world indiscriminately maimed and slaughtered the just and malevolent alike. Follows knew what mattered most was who survived, not who was just. The winners were freed to continue their lives, the losers lost everything. Fairness and honour contributed little to winning, deviousness and ruthlessness did; those were the world's laws.

The gods had sewn unfairness into existence by creating people unequal in strength, intelligence, family, and opportunities. The world did not protect the weak, it killed them first. It was man that imposed rules and systems to supplant this truth, but the world also punished man for such. Communal assistance reduced people's fear of failure and the incentive to better themselves. It succeeded in creating fewer exceptional individuals, and made people less defensive, until finally their group grew weak, and its collapse became inevitable.

He had not been encumbered, broken, and domesticated. He would not submit to anyone's ideal. He would discard order's oppressiveness; he would not be tamed; he would not bind his character. Tolerance was compromise and compromise damaged the spirit.

Under the silence, Follows shifted unsteadily towards the battleground's edge, each strained step watched by everyone. He stiffly stooped and retrieved his furs with pained fingers, his back shuddering. Slowly, he dressed under the stares and encouraging comments. He inhaled difficult breaths, enjoying the wind lifting through his hair and its cold upon his bruised body.

His next step parted the spectators and he exited through. Underneath the overcast sky, he walked towards the Chief and his destiny. Hare fell beside him, stunned and incredulous. Follows felt each gaze watch him leave and welcomed the notice, knowing his regard had been irrevocably changed. His actions were forever imprinted into hundreds of memories, his bravery indisputable and unforgettable, his momentum unstoppable. He had entered the fight a victim and emerged an intimidating power, just as he had intended.

TWENTY-THREE

SNOWFLAKES TUMBLED THROUGH THE frost-laden winds and speckled the men. Heavy snowfall was promising to visit and smooth the winter lands.

Follows carried himself from the combat ground, each stride soaked in ache. Cool breezes kneaded his face and neck, dimpling his skin and whispering to his ears. He stared upwards into the collecting darkness and welcomed its snows. Tonight, he would rest in his shelter, bathed by fire, and submerged beneath furs. Outside, the blizzards could beat upon the Settlement and break upon his hide walls, chorusing his reflections. He could indulge in his accomplishments and proudly enjoy his tiredness until sleep came.

Follows shifted through the snowflakes, Hare beside him, his spirit soaring with pride and achievement. Relief came easy, death chanced but escaped. Nerves and conflict had tired him, but purpose pulled him onwards. He looked at Hare, his hair dusted white, skin flushed with cold. Hare returned a solemn gaze, his shoulders sagged, his expression dejected and sobering. They walked beneath blackening clouds, sedately inspecting the other. Follows was confused by Hare's melancholy. He knew Hare disliked the Others, which forced his question.

'I know you resent the Others, Hare, why be downcast?'

'Resentment mostly impacts the resentful, but separation will impact entire families. No lands are as rich, the Others will fare worse outside them,' Hare said.

'Violence impacts more,' Follows responded. 'I've seen almost all my family killed or taken by others. They didn't care for us and were loyal to only each other. We can safeguard people from such trauma and seize peace for generations.'

Hare sighed and his gaze fell, his reply calm.

'My entire life I've watched the skies. I've learnt how to predict the coming weather, but I can't tell you what sky and clouds actually are. When young, I believed I knew, but now old, I know I don't. My youth emboldened me to claim wisdom I did not have, while age humbled me into uncertainty. No one knows what is right, but experience teaches you what's coming.'

'What weather's coming?' Follows asked.

Hare cast his attention skyward and examined the heavens.

'A storm,' he replied.

Despite his efforts and reason, unease infected Follows, turning his skin cold. An uncomfortable quiet pervaded. Their conversation died, and they became alone together. They walked silently, stiffened by cold as their furs and heads grew whiter.

The Settlement's corridors lay empty, everyone still behind them. Follows suddenly felt alone, rifted from people and friendless. The silent passageways echoed his feelings, successful but alienated, leading but alone. Yet he accepted it as part of his acquired position. He wanted only a partner to accompany his journey—a confidant for comfort and counsel. He hated his lonely nights and empty shelter. He knew isolation's pain and its humbling hurt, and knew its depression was always prowling and waiting to attack. Ambition could distract him, but old injuries were lifelong burdens always near. He needed to surround himself with family to deter loneliness and its desolation.

The weather was growing harsher, turning snowflakes into snowfall and breezes into gales. Winds churned the snows and blurred the ground, covering their feet and the distance in mist. They pulled hoods over loose hair and bowed their heads. Their steps became trudges and their hands disappeared inside mitts.

They left the Settlement and crossed the divide that separated the Chief, walked past his women's shelters, and arrived outside his large ornate home. Hare turned to Follows; ice interwove his beard, his eyes were tired, his eyebrows snow laden.

'Wait here, Wild One. The Chief must know my account is not influenced by your presence. Do not worry about duplicity, I have no agenda. I will recount impartially and inform the Chief the Settlement supports you.'

Follows held Hare's eyes, looking for deceit, but finding none. He trusted Hare and doubted he could lie convincingly. He signalled agreement and Hare nodded. The entrance was fastened closed, so Hare called through its folds.

'Chief, I have cause to speak with you.'

'I'd prefer to talk inside,' bellowed the Chief, laughing.

Hare lifted the entranceway and entered, leaving Follows alone collecting snowfall. He tucked his hands under his crossed arms and ignored the cold lashing his face. He rehearsed his proposals, his stare lost inside the gathering haze. Shivers crept over him but went unnoticed. He waited patiently under the arriving storm, snow thickening upon him, his thoughts abroad, until suddenly distracted. One of the Chief's partners emerged from her shelter, catching his attention. He watched her indifferently as she tied shut her shelter, but when she turned, he was overwhelmed.

She was clad in thick furs, but her female shape still seduced. Her hair lifted in the passing winds; her height approached his shoulders, her delicate features and skin faultless, her eyes an ethereal grey. She had only seen about fourteen winters, but nobody in the Settlement rivalled her. Her beauty was belittling, corrupting, hurtful. She stupefied and humbled, a cruel creation of the gods designed to haunt. How unworthy he felt, so flawed and comparatively dreadful. He was immobilised, feeling separated from the world and his situation. She had become the universe's centre, his ambitions trivial. His desire hurt and his old yearnings mauled him.

As she turned, she noticed him, and was stalled by his attention. She waited for him to speak but only silence came. She saw his attraction and it unnerved her. Without words to disperse the tension, she became uncomfortable, his desire intimidating. She was surprised by his open wantonness despite being the Chief's woman, feeling both sympathetic and anxious.

Snow lashed between their fifteen-pace divide, both rooted still—she by his inspection, he by her perfection. His coherence was elusive and words beyond reach. He could not look away nor summon expression, seemingly abandoned by his faculties. His wants sounded infantile, but he needed her, and any other woman would be a compromise. He noticed her discomfort and felt ashamed by his speechlessness, but finally he managed some words.

'What's your name?' he asked.

He saw her hesitate, presumably questioning their conversation's propriety. Slowly, she decided his question not inappropriate and replied, her voice wavering.

'Summer,' she called over the wind.

Their stares held, the silence smothering. Eventually the uncomfortable moments forced her away. She turned towards another shelter and left him watching helplessly. Her leaving hurt him, and he cursed his cowardice. He impulsively called to her, indifferent to consequence or embarrassment.

'Summer!'

She stopped and looked around, worried what he might do. He searched his feelings for words, filling the time with a terrible quiet. He stumbled over muddling thoughts and clasped for honest expression.

'Just seeing you has injured me,' he effused.

They quietly looked at each other, he impassioned and pained, she unsure how to proceed, both waiting for further words that never came. Finally, she turned away, and he forlornly watched as their gulf grew. She did not glance back as she approached and entered another shelter, abandoning him, stripping his vigour. He felt dejected and powerless, and languished dispiritedly until Hare interrupted him.

'Wild One, come meet the Chief.'

Follows' detachment broke, but his impetus was damaged. He strived to forget Summer and revive his plan's importance. He exhaled and it felt filled with pain. But he rescued some spirit when he remembered that power provides opportunities to manipulate circumstances; perhaps Summer was not lost.

He joined Hare, and they entered the enclosure together. He tied the entryway closed and stood respectfully awaiting invitation to sit. The room glowed and the walls rippled under the winds. The hearth threw out heat and the flames cast excited shadows. Furs draped the floor, and fire smoke wisped upwards, escaping through apertures into the darkening outside.

Across the fire sat the Chief, soaked in warmth, dressed in thick furs, eyes shadowed. Hare moved beside the Chief and sat by him, looking withdrawn, staring vacantly into the fire. The Chief inspected Follows over the flames, his face serious.

'Come sit,' said the Chief, his voice inexpressive.

The Chief beckoned Follows to some furs opposite him. Follows sat and waited, inspecting the austere Chief across the fire. The Chief had seen about forty winters. His inhuman stomach bulged beneath his clothes; his plump face reddened by firelight. The Chief's dark eyes travelled him, narrowed, assessing. Finally, the Chief spoke, his voice deep.

'I was told last night about the deaths on the cliff, Bear's accusation, your challenge, and the fight. But this conclusion was unexpected.'

The Chief looked saddened and sighed, and Follows heard his disappointment. The Chief continued, openly wearing regret.

'He was an honest man and his death a great loss,' the Chief said.

The Chief straightened, visibly burying his feelings behind immutable features, looking grave.

'Hare also told me about your speech, and the Settlement's support for your proposal to separate the groups,' the Chief said.

Follows composed himself and delivered his rehearsed counsel.

'Today the Settlement's divisions killed; they need to be eliminated to ensure peace. Your people support separation. Let me help you heal your fractured Settlement and return security. I understand your conflict: I have lived outside the Settlement where reality is not obscured, where survival means competing against others, often with fatal results. We must be vigilant and recognise threats to avoid this outcome. The Settlement has become complacent and abandoned vigilance, and lost the will to protect itself, hastening its demise. Living with the Others threatens both our futures. Both sides will prioritise their own interests, and each will advance and guard themselves over the other. Different languages and beliefs exclude outsiders, different customs ostracise others, and secluded enclaves discourage integration. These rifts damage cohesion and sculpt exclusive environments that prevent us all from growing freely. You cannot force assimilation without animosity and resistance. Therefore, the only solution is separation to avoid conflict. When the Others have moved, we will be free and safe. Only a unified people can combine their strengths and efforts to produce a stable future.'

The Chief's expression remained unchanged, disguising his feelings. A pause ensued, tensing Follows. The Chief disturbed the unease, his response impassioned.

'Your accent betrays that you are new here. Do not damage our peace with your ways, this is not the wild. What you propose could escalate. Once there was war and our sons died feeding it. Would you spill their blood again, and barbarise civilised people, and replace peace with atrocities, just to confront dangers which might never occur? We have outgrown force, we resolve issues diplomatically, prohibiting cause for revenge and feuds. Time will erase the Settlement's divisions. Our magnanimity will defeat rivalries and suspicions, and invite integration, eventually uniting us all, peacefully.'

The Chief's argument surprised Follows and stalled the discussion. The response was sincere but failed to address his arguments. The Chief's beliefs were idealistic but unrealistic, and beneath his eloquence, Follows sensed reluctance to entertain his beliefs. The human god believed inaction could cure the Settlement's divisions, and that confronting divisions was unnecessary and destructive. Yet eliminating threats had kept him alive—his life had proved it effective. He recomposed and readied his retort.

Inside the quiet the fire crackled, and over its flames the Chief held his stare. The world faded from notice, and Follows' concentration narrowed upon his opponent. His words broke the silence.

'People inherit their beliefs, identity, and customs from their family and community. Time grows divisions unless people abandon their old ways, and abandoning old ways removes that which binds groups together. The Others will multiply, compounding the divisions and resentments. Our contradictory interests will conflict, and there will be clashes, ending the peace you prize. If an invasion threatened to displace your practices and people, and take your resources, you would violently resist. Yet your land has been invaded and your people displaced, and no defence has been mounted. Either confine your people to erosion or defend their future.'

He finished, upset that their conversation had deteriorated into argument. He did not want to contradict the Chief, but censoring himself was counterproductive now. He wanted the Chief's support and knew the Settlement would not defy him. He needed to persuade the Chief, otherwise he could not stay in the Settlement; he would not live amongst rivals and risk himself or any future family.

The Chief discarded his composure and openly wore offence. The large man repositioned himself, inhaled, and launched into response.

'The Settlement was built in blood, ironically by dreams of peace. The echoes of conflict are still remembered. They embitter people and stifle reconciliation. No sophisticated leader would shatter peace to sully decent people in unpleasant acts. Peaceful resolution should be prioritised, otherwise violent reactionaryism will always prevent peace. Eventually, the Others will become fully part of the Settlement. We are not resisting an invasion. Conflict is not certain—both sides will compromise to better their lives, forging the groups gradually together, for tolerance breeds tolerance.'

Follows understood the Chief's sentiments, but knew his ideals disregarded human nature: man's territorialism, partisanship, competitiveness, and prejudices. These behaviours protected man, and forgoing them condemned him to weakness and displacement by those who embraced them. The Chief's ideas were built with unreal people and were contemptuous of the instincts which allowed man to survive. Perhaps the Chief's divinity made humans incomprehensible and their ways alien. Follows wanted to protect himself and confront threats; he would not abandon caution and safety for ideals.

Follows felt he was losing the argument; peace and inaction were easier to argue for than aggression and force. Yet he had to persevere; he could not return to the Settlement if it meant insecurity and cohabiting with potential enemy. He straightened, feeling drained, but his resolve unscathed. He cast aside his reserve and deferment.

'People don't change without incentive. You give away land and resources for nothing, hastening the Settlement's decline. Those without your ideals will conquer, making diplomacy and tolerance irrelevant. The same violence that fuelled your ancestors will revisit, and to pretend you are above violence is naive. Do not guard today at the expense of generations.'

The Chief's irritation was explicit, and any patience that had existed was gone. The Chief immediately replied, his tone dismissive and riled.

'I believe you suspect others of your nature. Hare says they even call you Wild One. With your divisive opinions and reactionary attitude, it seems too coincidental for three Others to accidentally die in your company. Without evidence, I cannot accuse you of deliberately killing anyone, but I know you are a threat to the Settlement, and I will ensure that you are ostracised and never have influence.'

Outwardly, Follows appeared calm but internally his loathing was building. The Chief was obliterating his ambitions and condemning him to insecurity and powerlessness. His advice and arguments had been snubbed by childish naivety, raising his fury beyond control. A fleeting silence passed before he exploded.

His rage propelled him to standing and hauled him over the Chief. He stood over the god, close enough to feel breath, feral eyes pouring hate. His hands and teeth clenched, his fists poised to strike. His violent behaviour sent alarm through the Chief and Hare, spearing them rigid. With wild abandonment, Follows rained his tirade upon the reeling Chief.

'I won't live under your foolishness. Men have tried to kill me instead of chancing my temperament, and I survived by killing them. And I'm grateful that my ancestors did likewise to ensure my existence. I've seen my family killed and taken by outsiders; I won't pretend the world is fair or kind. I'm not ashamed of my instinct to survive, but you are. So destroy your people without me. Your reality doesn't exist and never will. Your ideals condemn people's strength and applaud their weakness, time will not protect your kind. You were taught lies from childhood, and now you scorn truth because it contradicts those lies. But I choose truth. So enjoy your lies and captivity, I will not keep you company in your prison.'

Fear petrified the Chief, while Hare dared not move, his eyes fixed uncomfortably to the fire, despising his attendance. Follows could not bear the Settlement any longer; hopelessness was engulfing him. He felt his anger become hate, encouraging him to kill the Chief. But despite his loathing, a greater impulse seized him. He needed to escape the Settlement's madness and free himself. He turned and tore open the shelter's entrance and burst into the snowstorm.

Without pause, he violently strode through the deepening snows away from the Settlement. He would head for a hunting outpost to outwait the storm, then flee the area and consign it to the past and forget that he had failed again to live with people.

The snow struck him spitefully, scratching his face. He bowed into the currents, gritted his teeth, and hurled himself forwards, fuelled by disgrace and contempt. His gaze struck into the hidden distance, his body tensed, and the mists buried him inside their harshness.

TWENTY-FOUR

NESTLED IN CAVES NEAR the Settlement rested a dormant outpost, empty and still. The storm bellowed through its cavities, and snow tides crept into its entrance. The wind sang and surged outside, whistling and delivering cold.

From the snow and ice, Follows burst, crashing heavy steps onto the stone. His heavy breathing echoed around the cave as he shivered inside the dark. He pressed deeper, shaking hands outstretched, searching the blackness for wood and stone.

Slowly, the shadows surrendered their goods and allowed him to build a fire. With dulled fingers, he built a hearth and poured sparks over its tinder. Flames ruptured the gloom and assaulted the wood. The fire grew and chased away the night, spilling heat onto his cold skin. He shook himself of snow and undressed. He laid his clothes around the hearth, retrieved furs from the outpost's depths, and hunkered into them. He collapsed beside the fire and slowly nursed sensation back into his body.

Heaving and wading through the blizzard had crippled his energies, leaving him exhausted and near sleep, but despite his fatigue, his hate remained. Loathing drenched his thoughts and created vengeful fantasies. Even as his eyes closed, his feelings were malicious and miserable. But before sleep took him, a last coherent idea possessed him. He refused to suffer the destructive loneliness awaiting him—he could not bear its emptiness. After rest, he would return to the Settlement and take Summer. The blizzard would muffle her protests, and the snowfall would consume their tracks, secreting their escape until irretrievably distant. He would bound from outpost to outpost, and then vanish into the world's enormity, salvaging some triumph from defeat.

Resolute and committed, he let sleep take him. His head bowed and his arms fell; his body slackened and the world disappeared. Warmth soaked and caressed him as he slept. Outside, the storm wailed and whined, echoing around the cave, weeping as it brought death. Stillness returned to the cave, save the shimmying firelight climbing the walls. For a while, the cave rested peacefully, the fire burning, mellowing, and escaping as smoke into the outside winds. Then the peace was shattered.

Follows was shaken awake. Alarmed, he wildly looked for anyone or anything, but saw nothing. His sleepy mind was disorientated, but he surmounted his stupor, habitually seized his spear, and stood to fight. His disordered mind struggled awake as he dazedly scrutinised the cave and found it empty. Groggy but alert, he remained poised, wary, and inspecting, distressed by the unaccountable shaking that had woken him.

Uncomfortable moments laboured past; then he felt something. His feet tingled, then shook. Tremors crept up his legs and shuddered his body. He watched the fireplace tremble and a stack of spears shiver and fall. The entire world was shaking.

It took only a moment for him to understand. He had seen the world quiver once before, when Quiet had been fatally injured. His brother had returned, and he shook the world to signal it. Quiet's spirit had seen his misfortune and come to help him, and this realisation both weakened and elated him.

Follows ran to the cave's entrance, premonitorily knowing what he would find. Giant mammoths lumbered through the blizzard, shaking the ground and churning the snows. Awed and overcome, he watched them, overwhelmed that Quiet had forgiven him.

The memory he had strived to bury surfaced, bringing tears. He remembered the day he had killed his brother. The memory's agony was abhorrent and undiminished, crushing and engulfing, but the mammoths saved him from breaking. The herd was his brother's message of forgiveness, and a gift to help him exact revenge on the Settlement.

The man Follows loved most had returned to guide him, like countless times before. Their bond had transcended death and his transgression. He was euphoric. He felt his past and present all intertwining together to sew his future.

> *Four summers ago—the season was dying, the forests had reddened, and the winds were cool. The tall grasses were wet with dew and browning, and the days were growing shorter. The sound of water flowing over rocks sung through the trees; aurochs drank at the brook's shores, and the brothers advanced on them.*
>
> *They moved silently, the brook the only sound. Each step was careful and their movements slow. They hunkered low and moved gracefully between cover, closing on the grazing herd. Words were unnecessary, their actions symbiotic. They studied the herd, and agreed with a glance, on a nearby bull; then they readied for attack.*
>
> *But before they could attack, the ground momentarily trembled. Follows stalled, simultaneously stunned and doubting the experience. He looked at Quiet and saw his confusion, confirming it had happened. The brothers exchanged dumbstruck glances, but postponed discussion, reprioritising the hunt.*

They recomposed and continued through the knotted undergrowth, moving covertly to where their spears would not miss; but they never had the chance to attack. The ground quivered again and stopped them. The gentle tremors grew into quakes, upsetting their balance and rattling leaves from the trees. The aurochs raised scared eyes and quickly collapsed into panic. They began stampeding into the trees, escaping their hunters.

The brothers were frightened still. The earth shook and their bodies shuddered. Follows stood terrified, searching for explanation, unsure how to react. But the shuddering quickly ebbed into nothingness, leaving him motionless and bewildered, but vigilant and primed for confrontation. He listened but heard nothing. He speculated wildly, imagining the fantastical. He blamed gods and then invisible giant beasts, grasping for answers until suddenly interrupted.

He was tackled from his feet and thrown to the floor. His head snapped back and struck hard ground, darkening his awareness. Through the fog, he saw the figure that had attacked him, and his instinct lashed out. He repeatedly struck the figure and it retreated. But as his lucidity returned, the figure shed its shadow, and his brother appeared. As Follows dumbly questioned Quiet's attack, a large tree crashed onto where he had been standing.

Regret instantly seized Follows. Full of shame, he fell upon Quiet, apologising, attempting to embrace him. But Quiet was furious and pushed him away. Quiet raised himself, his brow and nose bloody, and staggered away. Follows watched, desperate to make amends, but unsure how. His composure faded, panicked at Quiet's anger. He called out to Quiet, hoping to stop him.

'I acted reflexively, I would never harm you,' he pleaded.

Quiet turned, his hurt expression streaked with blood.

'You are all I have, Follows, but sometimes you are a liability too impulsive to trust.'

The words wounded Follows. His throat clogged and his strength disappeared. He accepted the criticism without argument, desperate to avoid further hostility. Quiet walked away, and it was agony. Follows chased after him, begging forgiveness, but Quiet ignored every supplication. Follows persevered, trying to communicate his remorse, but Quiet was uninterested in resolution.

Every refused appeal humiliated Follows; each dismissal was demeaning, growing his misery. He continued until he grew resentful and aggravated. Anguished and indignant, he shouted at his brother, grasping for his attention, words cruel and exasperated.

'If you can't face your own brother, you're a coward. Maybe if you weren't such a coward, we would still have a mother and sister!'

His words injured even him. They were insincere and provoked by hurt, but they earned Quiet's attention. His brother faced him, eyes apoplectic, expression dark and violent. Follows had never seen Quiet wear such hate, and fear tore into him. He realised confrontation was likely, and panic drowned his clarity. He saw Quiet's spear and hate-woven features, *his tensed muscles and bowed head. He became torn between flight and defence.*

Then Quiet ran at him, bounds vicious, jaw and hands clenched. Horror seized Follows and he went rigid. Every moment carried his brother and his threat closer, dissolving his coherence. Hysteria ripped his sense apart. He forgot his brother and saw only approaching death, and his instinct reacted. Follows' spear left his hand and thumped into Quiet.

It punctured Quiet's upper chest and twisted him through the air. Quiet crashed onto the floor, limp and lifeless. Follows broke. He screamed. His shrieks infused with madness. His sanity disintegrated and his life fell apart. He crumpled to the floor, head in his hands as tears joined his screams, his chest feeling torn. He crawled towards Quiet, unable to stand or breathe, language gone, every faculty crippled. He pulled himself beside his motionless brother and heard his rasping breath. Quiet was comatose, eyes flickering, face contorted.

Follows snapped the stone from his spear and pulled the shaft back through Quiet. Despite his stupor, Quiet wailed, intensifying Follows' distress. When the spear was removed, Quiet lay inanimate and sweat soaked, breaths sharp and fast, mouth spilling saliva. Follows impulsively hugged his delirious brother, sobbing into his body. Quiet's blood spilled over them both, coating Follows' face, arms, and chest. His tears disappeared into the blood, his cries shivering and choked.

Blood-smeared and shaken, Follows took Quiet into his arms and stood. He carried him to the stream and laid him on its mossy banks. He placed him down as though an infant, afraid the smallest shudder would kill him. Follows ran into the forest to gather for a fire, fanatically determined to save his brother. He quickly returned, arms laden with wood, bark, and stone. He built the fireplace near Quiet and worked until it smouldered and ignited. He placed a spearhead beside it and bathed Quiet while the flames grew. Follows washed Quiet's blood away and cleaned his wounds for burning. Unable to stop the bleeding, he memorised the wounds between washes to ensure he treated them properly.

While the spearhead warmed, he fell into his brother's empty eyes. Their vacancy withered his strength and filled him with self-loathing. He knew only saving Quiet could save him. He retrieved the spearhead and began burning his brother.

Quiet moaned, each weep the frightening sound of a disconnected body. Follows singed closed the entry and exit wounds, then washed Quiet again. He rinsed away his blood and vomit, cleaned the wounds, and bound them. Quiet was deathly white, skin cold and damp. Follows unrolled some furs and wrapped him tightly inside them. He tried to get Quiet to drink, but he managed little without choking. Follows built a fire and hugged his brother, trying to impart more warmth.

He whispered to him, recounting their memories together, hoping their better times would revive his mind. He spoke about the fallen hatchling they had tried to raise as children, and their sadness when it died. He spoke about the snowman they had built and named, and how their family had eaten with it, then later ceremoniously bid it farewell when they departed. But his brother reacted to nothing. Quiet only shivered and convulsed, leaving Follows lost. Powerless to further help, he continued with stories, hoping somehow they would reach him.

As the sun descended and the day darkened, Follows continued to hold Quiet. He saw his delirium creep into fever as his skin grew paler, but hope kept him from breaking. Before night settled, he built a large fire in a nearby cave, and moved Quiet beside it. Follows succoured him with water, believing he was dragging him from death.

Through the night, Follows interrupted cradling Quiet to feed the fire, trying to deter the fever. At one point, Follows rose to drop branches into the flames, and as he returned, he saw awareness in Quiet's eyes. Ecstatic, he rushed to his brother. He stroked his face and lifted water to his grey lips, promising him recovery. The brothers held eyes, tears blurring Follows' vision.

Quiet was silent and his head lulled slightly. Follows saw no anger in Quiet, just sadness and disappointment. Their faces wordlessly spoke their tragedy and brought solemnity to the cave. With great effort, Quiet pried apart his lips and struggled to whisper. Follows neared, his ear almost touching Quiet, desperate to hear his voice. With laboured gasps his brother spoke.

'It is all chaos so we can be free,' Quiet murmured.

Follows waited for more but nothing came. Quiet only stared, heaving under strained breath, calm and exhausted. Traumatised, Follows embraced his brother, trying to hold him to the world, mumbling affection and assurances. He stroked his *hair, hopeful he might speak again, grateful Quiet had not left him. He held him until the fire began dimming. Follows rose to feed it and found Quiet lost again, adrift in fever. He fed the fire and then returned to hold him.*

Through the night, Follows never left his brother. He wordlessly guarded, unaware of hunger or tiredness. He roved through memories of their lives together, barely a day spent apart. Each recollection emerged more precious and desolating. But he could not escape this routine, and through the night he reminisced, and injured himself further.

Hunters from their group found them the next morning. Follows could manage neither words nor explanation, leaving the hunters to assume from nearby tracks that stampeding aurochs were responsible. The men fetched furs, food, and medicinal plants, and nursed Quiet, but eventually Follows' ugly mood drove them away. Follows' nerves were shattered and his ability to converse gone. His world was dying in his arms and nothing else existed.

He prayed and willed his brother better, but Quiet deteriorated. Over the succeeding days, his breaths grew shallower, his colour paler, his wound rotted, and his shivering increased. Follows never ate, he had forgotten himself. His life lost meaning and purpose, and he degenerated into a lonely creature barely attached to life.

On the third day, Follows watched Quiet's breathing slow to nothingness. His brother lay dead beside the fire, and he was alone. Haggard and careworn, Follows buried his brother. He moved hundreds of riverbed stones to the cave and covered his last family.

Without strength or impetus, he laboured all evening and into darkness. When the Moon rose and looked over the world, she saw Follows lying beside the stone grave, praying conflicting prayers to the gods—for his brothers return and to bless his afterlife. Mostly he begged Quiet's forgiveness.

The next morning Follows left the cave, hollow and fractured. He listlessly wandered into the forest for solitude, uninterested in life or recovery. He wallowed in nightmares and horror, terrified by life's fragility and brevity. Without anyone to share his memories, they seemed less real, and his past lost. Existence became trivial and inconsequential, dragging him deeper into hopelessness. He continued to deteriorate until he heard the senior man scorn his brother. Follows' anger had destroyed his detachment. That same day he butchered the senior man, and by night he was bounding for the Settlement, grasping for resurrection.

Follows never recovered, but life continued. Survival demands effort, and slowly, despite self-hate and tribulations, he rekindled his ambition and desire to live. Quiet's death would always damage his spirit, but he did find happiness again. The guilt would forever haunt him, but time accustomed him to its weight, and gradually freed him.

Follows never discovered the cause of the trembling earth, whether phantom beasts or gods, but the tremors that woke him tonight were undoubtedly his brother's doing. Quiet had used the events preceding his death to announce his return, knowing that Follows would understand. Quiet had returned to guide him, and he would follow.

Quiet knew that without purpose Follows was lost. Survival alone was meaningless; only ambitions inspire the spirit, and without them his character and drive would wither. The mammoths were Quiet's gift: an instrument to wrest success from his failure within the Settlement. He knew this true, and his certainty stoked his fervour.

He would kill the Chief and demolish the Others. Some of the Settlement would be destroyed, but Follows had no loyalty to the people, no shared ancestry and history. He was loyal to himself and owed himself fulfilment. He would seize the life he and Quiet had always wanted and seek leadership over whatever remained of the Settlement. The Chief had been weak; too restrained to kill him despite knowing him a threat. That weakness had endangered many, as Follows knew it would.

He disappeared into the cave and collected every spear, bound them together, and slung them onto his back. He then sprinted into the blizzard, ready to drive the herd into the Others. He would kill the Chief himself, and the prospect of fighting a god exhilarated and thrilled him. If he died, he would join his brother, if successful he would live in the Settlement without fear. The gods would decide his fate, and either outcome would satisfy him.

The effort of moving through the deep snows and freezing winds went unnoticed. He pursued the world's giants fanatically, elated his brother was nearby. Through the mist and snows he found the mammoths, and he raised a spear to steer them. Every movement felt momentous and predestined, and his success and safety assured.

TWENTY-FIVE

THE TEMPEST SCREAMED AND violently thrashed. He burst through the frozen world, every step immersed and sinking. Snowfall crashed into him, slashing at his eyes and unbalancing his strides, but his maniacal euphoria carved through the onslaught, unremitting and possessed.

His spears drove fear into the hindmost mammoths, rippling horror through the herd and coercing their stampede. His wild screams accompanied the pain he inflicted, chorusing the herd's progression from alarm into terror. The mammoths charged into the blizzard seeking escape, hurtling unawares towards the Others.

He impaled and speared, fanatically enthused, his determination implacable and savage. Soaked in rapture, he struck, his radicalism approaching ecstasy. His mind drowned in rhapsody, and his exaltation conquered exhaustion, summoning inhuman effort and strength. His mind was free, his aim was clear, and his destiny was tangible.

The herd was unusually large, likely a rare coalescence of herds. Mist secreted their number, but its spread suggested about seventy. This unstoppable weapon was indisputably his brother's doing, given with the gods' consent, their timely arrival too coincidental to believe otherwise. He wielded his brother's gift, its destructive potential chilling.

When the herd escaped, their trail guided him to them, and when reunited, he brutally reinvigorated their flight, never allowing their fright or momentum to lessen. When the mammoths were amongst the Others' shelters, the screams and panic would riot the herd and exacerbate the massacre. There would be no forewarning; the sleeping would never wake, and the storm would suffocate the cries.

The mammoths were close now, and the slaughter was certain. The foremost mammoth would already be amongst the Others' shelters, annihilating, some probably racing towards the Settlement. He launched his last spear into a frightened straggler, aggravating its hysteria, driving it into the herd, quickening its stampede a final time.

The last mammoths disappeared into the darkness. He raced after them, climbing and descending the hills surrounding the settlement. He ran across crushed snows, listening for anything but hearing only winds, looking for debris but finding only snow. The ground began shaking less, meaning the mammoths were growing distant.

He followed the pulverised ground until he found the destruction. Mangled and broken shelters had been flattened into graves, and their contents strewn into the snow. The dead were buried beneath trodden homes, and their blood carried in the wind. Contorted bodies and their expressions stole his fervency and slowed him. He walked through the ruin and desolation, past the mauled and lifeless, shocked but unrepentant, his act ordained by powers greater than himself.

Occasionally, dying cries found him, the pleading dreadful but not enough to weaken his resolve. He would persevere; he would never suffer loneliness, intimidation, or repression again. He would seek happiness without compromise, using any means.

He left the winter to silence the crippled; his priority was the Chief and Hare. Both their deaths were necessary, only they knew he might be responsible. He needed to be beyond suspicion, otherwise he could never return to the Settlement. He would claim the Chief had given him seniority to separate the groups, positioning himself to assume leadership. He could not be contradicted.

The Chief's shelter was likely spared by its separation, but the Settlement might be untouched, leaving Hare alive. He ran through the demolished shelters, bound for the Settlement. He needed no weapon, only his hands and strength to strangle and execute. He arrived in the Settlement, and quickly realised that the mammoths had obliterated it also. He had never intended this outcome and regretted it, but his part was easy to reconcile. The spirits and gods had delivered him the mammoths. They knew the outcome; he was just their instrument.

He journeyed through the wreckage, over blood-stained snows and rubble, his path interwoven with disfigured bodies and homes. Ice climbed the dead, and the blizzard buried the ruins, slowly hiding his massacre. He accepted the gods' ways. They acted through the strong—those willing to embrace action were the vessels of the universe's spirit and will.

He arrived at Hare's home. It was trampled flat and snow coated. He peered underneath its hides, looking for Hare, hoping the mammoths had finished him. He did find Hare, twisted and still, cold and dead. Despite his urgency, upset found him. The corpse was a mangled echo of the man. He had respected Hare and liked the Settlement's people, but he knew himself unable to appreciate the gods' plans, and so could never question their judgement.

He had to ignore guilt and continue; he was close to leadership, influence, and partnering with Summer; sentiment was a hindrance. He knew the gods rewarded the cunning, strong, and ruthless, and punished the weak, intransigent, and fearful; it was this intrinsic truth the Settlement had denied. Their greatest and final mistake was believing that tolerance would defeat the unscrupulous and merciless; perhaps their rejection of truth was why the gods had punished them.

Follows covered Hare in furs—a final ceremonial courtesy—then he beat onwards. He crossed the divide separating the Chief, his resolve absolute. The Chief's shelter emerged from the winter, frost lined and windswept. He paused outside the entrance to ready himself and ensure there were no witnesses, then charged into the shelter's darkness. His hands searched the gloom for his victim, grabbing and tossing aside loose furs. He circled the fireplace, fast and exact, narrowing upon the Chief's location.

Then he felt a man sat upright, awake but silent. The man's shape was round and soft, confirming it was the Chief. The Chief immediately challenged him, prideful and indignant.

'Who are you? How dare you enter.'

They were the Chief's last words. Follows gripped the Chief's throat and dug his thumbs into flesh. Follows' hands tightened and the other man thrashed. The Chief choked and writhed, impotently trying to escape, gasping for air he would never breathe. Follows suffocated him near unconsciousness, but before the Chief died, Follows leant close. He wanted the Chief to know his beliefs wrong before he passed into the next world.

'I am Wild One. We come from different places. Yours killed you.'

They were the last words the Chief would hear. Finally, the Chief's resistance subsided, and he turned limp. Follows heaved the Chief onto his shoulders and waded into the Settlement. He would hide him amongst the destruction and claim the mammoths responsible. He strained under the weight, pushing through the snows, then discarded him; another victim of the massacre the morning would reveal. He retrieved a large stone and caved in the Chief's head, masking his inflictions, making the stampede the obvious culprit.

He abandoned the stone far away and returned to the Chief's shelter, where he would wait to be found. He had already been championed by the people, and once found in the Chief's home, his authority would be further strengthened. No danger remained; morning would begin his rise. He could rest and plan his leadership. His brother would be near, protecting and ensuring his success. He whispered gratitude, overcome with affection.

The blizzard whipped against his furs and the winds lifted through his hair. The Wind God accompanied him, encouraging and supportive of his undertakings.

TWENTY-SIX

INSIDE THE GLOOM AND warmth, he drifted between sleep and wakefulness, nervous but excited, restless despite his tiredness. He waited for interruption, imminently expecting people seeking their Chief. He rested beneath furs, enjoying the quiet and reflection. The blizzard assaulted the outside, but the Chief's home protected and blanketed him in warmth and calm.

Through the shelter's apex, he watched the morning lighten. White skies and snows grew visible, and interruption closer. He shut his eyes against the dawn, enjoying the rest the day would disallow. He drifted through thoughts and plans, but became fixated on the God Chief; his killing had been too easy. How could a god be so fragile? He ruminated until the truth assaulted him. He realised the gods and spirits had assisted him, and that all his recent seasons had been planned and part of this eventual outcome. He remembered all his prayers and conferences with the Wind God, asking for assistance and guidance, and his god had answered those prayers.

When his brother had died, the Settlement had saved him. While alone, he had survived men and Neanderthal, unknown lands, winters, and predators. When debilitated by loneliness, Mane had rescued him from despair, and reinvigorated his spirit and strength. Her death had reawakened his determination and resolve. He had found the Settlement, but his past and experiences had prevented contentment, stirring him to action. Then his brother had returned to deliver the mammoths, and finally, a god had died easily in his hands.

Seeing that his life had been planned was humbling, the gods' inhuman foresight intimidating. The gods' plans were indiscernible until complete, too intricate for human notice. These realisations were overwhelming, elevating his devotion to the Wind God, making him more aware of his humanity.

He lay awed and impressed until finally disturbed. The entranceway was thrown open and a woman fell upon the furs covering him, frantic and loud, shaking him, calling him Chief. Follows surfaced from the furs with pretended surprise. The woman fell backwards, shocked, expecting the Chief. She was probably one of the Chief's women, her face engraved with panic and anguish. They inspected each other, eyes questioning.

'Who are you? What are you doing here and where is the Chief?'

'I am Wild One. I counselled late with the Chief, discussing the Settlement's future, and he invited me to stay. I don't know where he is, but during the night the ground shook, and he may have gone to investigate.'

He raised himself, outwardly grave but internally pleased, his fictitious bond with the Chief was witnessed, and his claim to authority evidenced. He strode towards the entrance, past the woman, she staring and indecisive. He requested her company.

'Let's find our Chief.'

Not knowing how to react, the woman followed. They entered the early morning; the sky was hidden behind grey heavens, and the world was sombre and colourless. Light snowfall fell and he shivered under the winds as they crossed the divide and entered the Settlement.

Without darkness, the Settlement's wretchedness was naked

and horrific. The disfigured dead lay collecting ice. Faces were frozen and pained, and the shelters torn and bloody. He stepped amongst the carnage and contorted people, dazed by the massacre's totality. The snows were claiming his victims and burying the lifeless. Ruptured bones pierced blue skin, devoid eyes stared into nothingness. He was stunned by the annihilation, still and dazed, until the woman recaptured her voice.

'Mammoths destroyed us,' she cried brokenly.

He looked at the woman, her cheeks tear-streaked, her despair wounding. They stood inside the dreadful silence, by pummelled shelters and stiffened people, stalled by the gruesomeness. The Settlement was irreconcilable with memory, its community gone, its shelters now tombs. The stampede had been unforgiving, and he wondered how many people remained. The woman's face was harrowed and her sobbing fierce, but he needed her help, so he spoke confidently to rally her.

'Gather the Chief's women and search for people. Assemble any survivors at your shelters and we'll house them,' he said.

The woman stared at him, his collectedness contrasting her discomposure, his orders providing her purpose amidst hopelessness, stirring her to adherence. Silently she left, her downcast steps slowly sinking her into the fog. He watched her sympathetically but knew she would recover, time accustomed people to their traumas. He had recovered after Quiet and Mane had died, and so would time repair her.

He explored the deserted wastelands along known trails now unrecognisable, looking for the familiar, but finding only devastation. Soon the Chief's women arrived and helped him search the winter desert. Summer was amongst them, incomparably beautiful despite her melancholy. Their eyes met momentarily, his interest inconcealable despite his efforts. She severed their glance and guiltily looked away. Despite the situation, seeing her was still uplifting and intoxicating. Authority without her would be empty.

Follows and the women did find people, impossible chance had spared some shelters. Their traumatised occupants were stranded amongst the chaos, wandering the ashes of their lives dispiritedly looking for family and friends. He approached them with real tenderness and invited them to the Chief's shelters. They fixed him with glazed eyes, but they followed. Gradually, he separated every survivor from the bloodshed, and collected them at the Chief's grounds.

A returning hunter informed him thirteen men were still abroad, letting him know the remaining population. Twenty-three women, nineteen men, and sixteen children lived; near five hundred had died. No Others remained. Later, a woman found the Chief—his discoloured body rigid with frost, his crushed head collecting snowfall—exacerbating people's despair and savaging their hope.

With several others, Follows began disassembling intact shelters and reassembling them at the Chief's area, slowly housing together the living and abandoning the Settlement to the dead. The morning passed and the snowstorm continued, but he worked relentlessly. By evening, the temporary camp was finished. Shelters for each family and individual were afforded so grief could be uninhibited, and those needing company could share sorrow. Already people approached him for leadership, his headship unspoken, but unconsciously accepted.

As darkness stained the sky, broken people sought solitude inside their new homes. Fires grew and defeated the colds, protecting the tired and cheerless. Smoke wisped into the winds and firelight coloured the shelters' walls. Meats were cooked and sleep was sought but barely glimpsed.

Before Follows returned to the Chief's shelter to rest, he visited those awake. Each conversation differed, but his reassurances varied little. He commiserated unreservedly, his sympathy genuine despite his responsibility. The survivors echoed his agony for his dead family, their helplessness and dejection painfully recognisable. Empathetically, he promised to rebuild their lives and provide support and stability. He vowed to continue the Settlement and ensure the living rebirth and prosperity. Most were too detached to engage with him; some thanked him. None challenged his leadership—everyone was too delicate.

When he had finished visiting people, he exited into the night, dragged slow by tiredness. Yet there remained a final shelter to visit, and he carried himself there. Snowflakes settled upon his weary head and shoulders, his spirit solemn and thoughts sober. Overhead, the Winter God ruled the world, showering the land with blizzards and ice, churning snows and attacking life. But he doubted the Winter God even noticed him. To gods, humans and their greatest undertakings must seem trivial.

He exhaled sleepily as he watched his breaths whisk towards the infinite above. He looked up into the heavens, its stars hidden behind overcast skies. His mind wandered the future—dreams of influence and family, of women and glory, of old age and legacy. Those left alive would restore the Settlement's practices and structures and return stability—except now he would lead. Today's catastrophe would become memory, and time would distance its pain. He would relocate people and spare them reminders of the disaster and their pasts. While winter reigned, he would bury the dead and disguise the Settlement's remains, so that when the snows rescinded, its memory would not burden people.

He arrived at Summer's shelter, its entrance folds glimmering crimson and seeping firelight. Despite his fatigue, nervousness gripped him, quickening his beating chest, and upsetting his composure. But he ignored his worry and called to her.

After a few breaths, the entrance opened, spilling warmth onto him and light into the dark. Summer knelt before him, silhouetted against the bright interior. Their eyes met, hers cautious and his naked. Difficult moments passed, the correct words elusive and his enchantment embarrassing. She searched him, contemplative and assessing. Her eyes were reddened from recent tears, yet she was controlled.

He knew she was afraid of the future and her vulnerability; she was unprotected and at the mercy of charity. But despite her grief, she was self-possessed, and perhaps aware that he could provide the protection the stampede had stolen. Her partner and family were gone, and the world's dangers threatened, forcing her practicality. His interest and emerging leadership were desirable—a shield against privation and mistreatment—and she wore her pragmatism despite her tragedy. She disturbed their silence.

'You may come in and talk awhile,' she told him.

She disappeared inside; he entered the fire-lit enclosure and tied closed its entranceway. She sat upon her fur bedding and gestured he sit opposite her. They inspected each other across the flames, he imposing but uneasy, she distraught but dignified.

The fire swayed and crackled above the quiet but could not distract them. She waited for him to speak; his visit required explanation despite its obviousness. Tense, but honestly, he spoke.

'Partner me. You will not want or fear again. I will support you without reservation, and care for you without diminishment,' he confessed, uncaring of embarrassment.

He waited, watching her reaction, vulnerable to her response. He saw her thoughtfulness, instinctively hesitant and unwilling to commit so quickly. She was unsure of his character and dependability, yet she saw loyalty and affection. Without him she was defenceless, and dependent on altruism amongst disorder.

'I would like that,' she quietly replied, her voice hopeful despite its sadness. 'But let's proceed slowly. I have lost my family and partner; my recovery and affections won't be immediate. But if you are patient and kind, I will give you my trust and gratitude.'

He listened, impressed by her bravery and self-possession. He had been incapable of such composure when his family had died. He felt increasing tenderness and admiration for her.

'I will be patient, I want nobody else,' he told her gently. 'I have also lost everyone I've ever cared for. The world takes what it gives, but it doesn't have to be lonely.'

He finished, feeling unburdened by his candour, and hopeful he had assuaged her doubts. He saw relief behind her upset, and premonitorily felt a long affiliation beginning. Tiredly he stood and nodded farewell, his smile weary but friendly and hers the same. She watched him untie the entrance and leave, but as he stepped outside, she asked his name.

He turned. He knew his response. He was Quiet's brother, no matter the company or place, past or future.

'I am Follows,' he told her, and she smiled.

Uplifted, he exited into the storm, sealed the entranceway, and carved through the snows towards rest. He sunk into the night, alone but not lonely, knowing his brother was near, and that Summer would share his future.

TWENTY-SEVEN

THE LONG DARK WINTER days passed slowly as the Winter God ruled unsympathetically, assaulting with storm and blizzard. But as the Winter God exerted himself, the Sun God rested and readied to defeat his rival.

Gradually winter's ferocity lessened, the days lengthened, and the Winter God was driven from the world. He took his snows, and the Sun God brought his warmth. Colours poured into the reviving world, and grasses emerged from the disappearing snows. The land blossomed, animals awoke, and survival grew easy.

The Settlement's survivors had worked together through the winter to rebuild their lives. Living demands effort, and effort mends damaged people. Tasks had distanced people from their tragedies and bonded them, creating a cooperative culture that chased away loneliness. Most remaining men and women partnered and recaptured some of their stolen comforts, and even those beyond repair could not impede the group's rebirth.

He had built a Settlement from the broken fragments of people. Hunters roamed, fishermen sailed, and fires burned each night as people concluded their days together. His leadership had been unopposed and natural. When the snows had vanished and the breezes blew warm, his headship was indisputable.

During the winter nights, he and Summer had grown close. Their tentative beginnings became slowly intimate as needs united them. Affection followed, and she fell pregnant, and his life finally approached contentment. But there remained a curiosity he could not ignore. When the world had thawed, no excuse remained to delay its exploration.

His boat drifted over the gentle sea as summer's warmth surrounded him. The clear blue sky promised a calm voyage and allowed his mind to drift. The wind graced his skin and lifted through his loose hair, his old friend always watchful and accompanying.

He sailed for Salt's new world. People had tried to dissuade him, but time had strengthened his obsession. Every day he had imagined the fantastical possibilities beyond the world's borders and been tormented by his ignorance. He could not grow old never knowing what those lands held, or live suspecting himself of cowardice.

Regardless of success and time, he planned to reunite with Summer. His curiosity would be appeased and knowing would unburden him. He could discover paradise or ruin, be stranded, or return quickly—fate would decide.

Obstacles had to be conquered to better lives. Comfort and security dissuaded people from risk, but they also weakened them. Man had wandered for countless generations and been shaped by impermanence, making his nature restless and novelty seeking. Settled life was systematic and predictable, lessening the world's majesty and beauty. It caused people's imagination and excitement to suffer, and without new experiences they withered. A journey grew and strengthened the person, the destination was only the impetus. Routine buries wonder and repetition bores, stealing motivation from people, limiting their development. Rooted communities restricted people's personalities and demanded conformist characters and opinions. The compensation was security, but it was novelty that inspired.

The world demands payment for everything: sacrifice for freedom, and freedom for security. People's fear decided their life. The unknown was intimidating and promised nothing, limiting the existences of the afraid. Man was rational but his feelings were not. Sense chose security, the spirit sought freedom and the unknown. Man's duality tore him between the familiar and his wildness—one quality protected him, the other contented him. Despite many seasons of suffering and loneliness, he missed the wilderness's chaos, harshness, and beauty. Nature had raised him and made him in its image.

He knew the gods had sewn disorder into their creations to prevent them stagnating. The Settlement had tried to suppress that disorder to keep peace, but that had weakened them. Competition, hardship, and ambition motivated and kept man strong. Not all could triumph, otherwise nothing could have value.

The Settlement had incarcerated man and limited the depth of his existence, but he doubted such cohabiting systems could survive indefinitely. The disorder in people would always build instabilities until collapse became inevitable. Violence was momentary and its effects permanent, making peace forever impossible.

He understood the world, and knew only his strength and cunning guaranteed him freedom and survival. The Settlement had been destroyed because it was weak. It had believed it was protected from the world's unruliness and cruelty because it was fair and considerate. If the Settlement had been less accepting, or the Chief willing to exterminate threats, both would still be alive. But had the Chief killed him, he would have had to acknowledge that Follows' instincts protected better than his ideals and tolerance.

Ultimately, who was wrong or right, or just or underhanded, mattered less than who survived. Follows was alive and full of hope, free to explore and resist compromise. He did not know if god, man, or animal lay beyond the world's edge, but it was unimportant, for the rules that governed the living invaded every recess under the sky. What he knew was true and would be true forever, wherever he arrived.

'The world takes what it gives, indifferent to the lives it holds. We are born into struggle, collide with others, and are coerced by our environment. But we defiantly stumble on, struggling against obstacles and mortality. We are humbled by our limitations, ruled by desire, humiliated by our failures, burdened by tragedies, and forced to accept our own impermanence. The world steals our certainty and purpose, and leaves us accepting a life never planned, while ageing pulls us towards an end once unimaginably far away. Eventually we will be forgotten.

'But our assigned time affords us the opportunity to fight, and although our ends are predetermined, the chance to chase ambitions, resist restrictions, and defy limitations are our greatest freedoms. Our existence is tragically brief, but despite our transience, our struggle has purpose; only when we cease struggling are we defeated. In this life, strength is a choice.'

ABOUT THE AUTHOR

James Walker is a chartered nuclear, mining, and mechanical engineer, and a former infantry and signals soldier, with various degrees in physics and engineering. He has worked on nuclear submarines, nuclear weapons and reactors, in construction and manufacturing, and now works in the mining industry. James was born in South Africa, grew up in England and Cyprus, and now resides in Canada.

Above Instinct was inspired from soldiering for protracted periods alone in the wilderness, and the symbiotic and anthropomorphic relationship that naturally develops with nature.